To !

Yes, I rea

Love

Ba

Bay Clan

9/1000

Black Pepper Special Editions
Black Pepper First Edition handsigned
and numbered by the author

RUNNING DOGS

RUNNING DOGS

RUNNING DOGS

BARRY KLEMM

Black Pepper

First Published by *Black Pepper*
403 St Georges Road, North Fitzroy, Victoria 3068

National Libary of Australia
Cataloguing-in-Publication data:

      Klemm, Barry
      Running Dogs
      ISBN 1 876044 31 4

      I. Title

A823.3

Cover designed by Gail Hannah

 This project has been assisted by
the Commonwealth Government
through the Australia Council,
its art funding and advisory body.

Printed and bound by Arena Printing & Publishing
35 Argyle St, Fitzroy 3065

Black Pepper books are distibuted by Dennis Jones & Associates
19A Michellan Court, Bayswater, 3135.
Tel: 03 9720 6761. Fax: 03 9720 4472.

ACKNOWLEDGEMENTS

Several chapters of this novel have previously been published:
"River of Gold" in *Australian Short Stories* #37 in 1992;
"Buddha's Day Off" in *Australian Short Stories* #42 in 1993;
and again in *Fabulous at Fifty* (Cafe Publishing, 1995).
"Perfect Timing" was runner-up in the Weary Dunlop Award, 1996.

The events of this novel took place between April 1967
and March 1968 in Phouc Tuy Province, South Vietnam.

*Not only can we now say that the enemy cannot win but we ourselves
have won the war although it is not yet at an end.*
General Westmoreland, U.S. Commander in South Vietnam
April 1967

The Tet offensive has meant nothing less than defeat for the enemy.
General Westmorland, March 1968

LIST OF CHARACTERS BY RANK

BATTALION: 7th BATTALION – nicknamed Pig Battalion
Porky, Colonel – Battalion Commander/Lieutenant
Haig, Captain – Intelligence Officer
The Beast, RSM
Ky, Vietnamese Interepter

COMPANY: DELTA
Hatrack, (Major Alexandar Haddon)
Bulldog Doyle, CSM
Wilkins, Signallman / Private
Davidson, Medic / Private
Modlin, Tom, Staff Sergeant, Quartermaster
Martin, Payclerk / Private

PLATOON: 11th
Holly, (Peter Hollingsworth) Lieutenant
Braddock, Sergeant, called Skull
Lawson, Sergeant Henry
Ten Days, Corporal, Medic
Mumbles Dorset, Signallman / Private

SECTION: 4th
Nigel, (Robert) Naughton, Corporal
Dunshea, (Albert, Albie), Lance Corporal
Snowy Spargo, Gunner / Private
Sniffer, (Terry) Gibson, Scout / Private
Griffin, (Yogi, Bear, The Bear), Private
Greyman, (Billy Goolie), Private
Bugsy Norris, Private
Micky Wright, (Replacement), Private
Daytripper, (Replacement), Private

6th SECTION:
Andy Kinross, Corporal

1. River of Gold

Even before Sniffer came back too soon, you knew you were in the shit. You got it in the fuckin' neck—early warning system: it happens like that sometimes. Not always: that's the fuckin' trouble. Just sometimes.

You're sitting there, back up against a tree with your nose stuck up a stick book—thumb in your bum and your mind in neutral—when all of a sudden you're rubbing the back of your neck, like some fuckin' insect bite only it don't sting. Just tingles. You rub it and then, you realise.

Trouble...

Now the tingling gets into them hairs at the nape and you know it's on. You look up, the last words you read already forgotten.

Nothing...

Nothing...

You look toward the way Sniffer'll come but he ain't there yet. Look the other way. You can see Snowy through the lightspeckled shadows, twenty feet away, flanked by the gun, and Alby Dunshea further over. Nothing there. You know the others are beyond. No sign of them.

Nothing.

Fuckin' nothing.

Swing back round. Bugsy lies beside you with his hat over his eyes, sound asleep? Nope. He's absently rubbing the back of his fuckin' neck! Now he lifts the hat an inch off his eyes and peeps out to see if you've got it too. Yeah, Bugsy, I got it too. Has to be Sniffer. Has to be. You peer back that way. A few clear feet of shadow under the canopy of the jungle and then a hell of a tangle of green shit, but there's a gap you can see through at this angle, right down. Not so

1

far as the sentry post, but far enough. Wait for it. Wait for it. There he is!

Sniffer comes creeping back through the greenshit, real quiet, well in from the track. He stops, bends, peers—he's trying to spot you. You move your arm a few inches—all it needs. His eyes pick it up, and he stoops a little more so you can see his face but in all that shadow and shit you can't make it out clear—he's still twenty yards away. But that's enough. Very methodically, Sniffer holds his fist right in front of his face with the thumb pointing upward and then turns it over, slowly and deliberately, so the thumb points down—just like the Roman Emperor does at the Colosseum and it means the same fuckin' thing too! Sorta. It's the signal for enemy approaching.

You give the same signal back, and keep watching him close, while Bugsy is watching you and sees the reply. He immediately offers the thumbs down signal along the line to Snowy and Alby Dunshea— they aren't fuckin' looking. Bugsy finds a small twig and throws it their way. Now he can pass the signal and they will pass it, on to Nigel and Greyman who are further over that way somewhere. All this you are only vaguely aware of, sensed at the periphery rather than seen—you are concentrating on Sniffer.

When he sees you've got the signal, Sniffer, very emphatically, shows four fingers on one hand, then one with the same hand. Four of them, maybe one more. Okay. You pass that signal on to Bugsy who sends it down the line. There's another possible signal that doesn't come—a pumping of the fist like someone in the latter stages of wanking a giant prick. It means they're right on top of you and you're in a hurry. But Sniffer makes no such signal. Plenty of time. Sniffer now settles down where he is, ten yards in from the track. Time to move.

Carefully, you slip your stickbook into your pack and fasten the clips—set to bug out fuckin' quicksmart if necessary. Then you shove off the tree, pick up your SLR and crocodilecrawl forward a couple of yards to a place aligned with Bugsy but about five yards toward Sniffer's position from him. Check it carefully. Clear view of Sniffer from here, clear the other way to Bugsy, and beyond the vague outlines of Snowy and Dunshea. Moving slowly, you check your SLR— full mag, one up the spout, safety off. Check your pouch for extra mags, the other for the grenade if that's needed. All set. Let's have yer, you little slant-eye bastards!

You settle into your prone position, the ground is cold on your belly and thighs but that's alright. Bare earth means not much fall-out from the trees to crunch and crinkle. Means you can see any fuckin' snakes or scorpions coming too, thank fuck! Means you've got good footing if you have to move. You manoeuvre again, a few positioning wriggles to get comfortable, get your elbows onto smooth ground so the nerves won't be jarred, and all the time ensure clear view of Sniffer one way and Bugsy the other. From Bugsy's direction comes the common 'okay' signal—thumb and forefinger pulled into a circle. Everyone ready. No probs. Sniffer is settled, Bugsy is settled—time to concentrate on the track.

The track is narrow and winding through the greenshit, at this point ten yards directly up front. Here the jungle is dense, dank and dark, but over the track the canopy is breached and sunlight comes through illuminating the track so that it kinda flows through the dimness like a river of gold. Out there, you can see everyfuckin'thing that moves—it's like a lighted stage waiting for the actors to walk on—and just as an actor on a brightly lit stage can't see the audience, so too from the track, we are completely fuckin' invisible.

You tried it yourself earlier—stood out there and looked right where Snowy was, and saw fuckin' nuthin. All we have to do is stay still and no one would ever know we are here. That's the skill of an ambush, to see without being seen. They could never detect you in a million years, but we will have a bright clear unobstructed view of them. They've got fuckin' buckley's.

We're good at this. Watch how surely it is done. You look back toward Sniffer: he is down and motionless, watching the track—for sure he expects them to appear right away. At some distance now, you hear the ringing sounds of what might be bird-calls, but they ain't. No fuckin' fear. They are the voices of people calling light-heartedly. It sounds like a discordant song. Definite Vietnamese. You

3

lie there, sweating it out.

There is a tremulous feeling rippling through your body, a feverish anticipation, like a child about to receive a Christmas present. The sweat breaks out on your brow, your neck, the palms of your hands, that same cold sweat that comes with nausea. Your belly dislikes the hard contact with the damp earth; you need to shift your knees slightly, you tense and flex the muscles in your legs and back to keep them supple, tighten the buttocks and free them. It's like fucking the ground itself. You have to remember to breathe as well, for the tendency is to hold the breath. You seem to have slipped your entire body into manual drive. Nothing happens unless you consciously will it. And it is all focused, channelled, into the eyes and the ears. You must concentrate on that track. Nothing else matters.

The ringing voices are nearer. You are locked in, the trap straining against itself to be sprung. Check back with Sniffer—he's watching for you. Again, he raises four fingers—a confirmation. You pass the signal to Bugsy—rugged, rough Bugsy, but now his florid face is pallid and strained as, you must suppose, your own is. Certainly the four fingers you display are trembling. Back to the fuckin' track, concenfuckingtrating. Where are they? Where the fuck are they? There!

They are visible for just a few seconds, but at such moments, time slows down and you see and hear and feel everything in minute detail, like a slo-mo replay only it's for fuckin' real. They come hustling along in their short-stride gait, chatting in sing-song Noggie as they go. The actors, entering stage left, each weighed down by a disproportionately ponderous load. Actors never really work that fuckin' hard.

The man in the lead is barechested and barelegged, with ricetubes looped about his torso and he has an enormous bundle of straight sticks on his back, longer than he is tall, bending him forward as he moves. He carries an AK47 cradled on his forearm. You can pick it from the curved magazine and your eyes light up. Nasty little buggers, them.

A woman, his wife perhaps, follows in black pyjamas and straw

4

hat. She too is stooped under a huge bundle wrapped in black plastic and carries a .303 slung on her shoulder. She grins sweetly as she chats with the two younger men behind, her cherubic cheeks etched by shadow.

The younger men are lightly built and sinewy—maybe her sons. Both labour under the weight of US ration boxes lashed to their backs. One carries a shotgun, the other a US M1.

All that you see in the first second. You absorb it from a single fleeting moment, and you will never forget it. The first second passes since they hustled into view, and in another second they will be gone. It must be now. And yet, for all their speedy gait, they seem to pass so slowly, caught in a time warp, waiting for death. Without missing a stride, the lead man turns and says something and they smile at his comment, thinking it funny. They will die with those smiles on their lips.

The last man in line is yours. Yours and Sniffer's. Your SLR is at the shoulder but you don't use the sights. You'll start behind and walk the tracers onto him, while Snowy hits them in the guts with his beloved Mabel, taking them all on while we pick off individual targets. Sniffer, accurate shot, will go for one killer hit on your target, while you blast all around him, giving him nowhere to go. Now! Do it now! Go Snowy...!

Snowy lets Mabel have her way. At the moment they draw level with him, he gives them a solid fifty round burst. All four are hurled to the far side of the track as if struck by a great wind, crashing to the ground in a flurry of flailing limbs. Bright horizontal streaks of tracer sear across the track and into their thrashing bodies, showering the track with a hail of twigs, leaves, splinters, dust and smoke. All is obscured, mercifully, except that the woman's piercing scream can be heard above the thunder of the gunfire, until she stops as if cut off by a knife. The barrage ceases as suddenly as it began.

It is all over in three seconds flat. You've fired a full mag into that last guy, although you saw little of him after the firing began. Everything vanished momentarily in a frenzied fog of smoke and dust and leaf fragments and splinters, and when it cleared they were down.

You knew where he was and sent your bright stream of tracers zeroing into the spot, until the mag ran out. It takes a moment to remember to stop squeezing the trigger. Take a breath of air. Quick change the fuckin' mag, fuckwit! Whip it off, whip it out, whip it on, click! One up the spout, whack, whack! All neatly done in spite of numb and trembling fingers. Okay. Now check upfront. All you can see out there is your target, down and thrashing on the ground. That's all you have to see.

As the echo of the gunfire stalks away through the jungle, there is a brief lull. Then come the voices of the victors: sharp, callow voices, all calling at once.

"Aw, you bloody bewdy, Snowy..."

"We got 'em...we got 'em..."

"You fuckin' balltearers..."

"Bowled 'em right arse over tit..."

"Did yer see 'em drop..."

"That'll take their fuckin' minds off sex for a while..."

Then, the more mature voice of Nigel. "Awright, awright, shut up, you dickheads!"

The dreadful lull returns. Hate this. But you gotta be sure. No point taking chances. Everyone stays where they are, weapons trained on the bodies, waiting for something, anything. Nothing moves now. The death throes are over.

"Awright, take it easy. Watch 'em," Nigel is saying unnecessarily—his voice has that same hysterical edge to it. "Sniffer, that the lot?"

Nigel is invisible at this distance, calling just loud enough for Sniffer to hear him.

"Yeah, just four."

"You okay?"

"Fine, Nigel."

"What's up with you, Alby?"

"Got a heap of shit in the face but I'm alright."

"Can't make you any fuckin' uglier."

"Stick a dick in it, Yogi Bear!"

6

"I take it you're still with us, Griffin."

"I'm here, Nigel."

"Bugsy."

"Yo?"

"Gun clear, Snowy?"

"Gun clear, Nigel."

"Greyman!"

"No problems, Nigel."

"We got four victor Charlie down. Who can count 'em."

"I can count 'em," Bugsy calls. "Four Charlie down and out."

"Awright. Check weapons. Reload. Stay where you are."

Oh gawd, is he gonna ask me? Please, not me. I don't like this, never want it. He reckons I'm good at it, but I don't feel good at it. Just don't shit myself if it goes wrong.

"Griffin, wanna have a look?"

Oh, fuck it!

You groan in response. You let that be the answer. There's a snort of amusement from Bugsy, and then Nigel. "You don't have to do it, Yogi."

Oh, sure you don't! Then some other poor fucker goes out there instead and goes cunt up and it's all your fault. Fuckin' wonderful.

"I'll do it."

"Play it cool, Yogi Bear. We got all day."

Like fuck we have. Every Charlie within ten miles in any direction now knows exactly where we are, and there are no sentries. When you're out there, you're all on your own, baby.

You roll onto your side—have to anyway because you've got a bloody erection and its getting fuckin' uncomfortable under there. You bring your SLR around where you can check the mag, ensure the spout is clear and there's one up there, make sure a spare mag is ready. The SLR is a good gat but the barrel's too long for this sort of job—some blokes lop the muzzle but that kills the accuracy and increases the muzzleflash—no win situation. Maybe you oughta carry a pistol on your belt, except someone'll think you're an officer and you'll end up getting fragged. Right now, the SLR will have to do.

You look at Bugsy but he concentrates on those inert forms out there, his rifle trained. Take your hat off—dump it on the ground, check the machete on your belt. Slide it in and out. Set to go.

You take your time. Slowly you get to your feet, and then look toward Sniffer down the way. He gives the thumbs up. Okay. No fancy stuff now. You stand full upright, and walk slowly, straight forward, and straight away that fuckin' long barrel tangles in the vines. You pull it free, steady your nerves, and all the way you watch those bodies, nothing else. As long as they don't move, there's no problem. At the edge of the track, you pause, wait, watch. Then, finally, you step out in to the sunlight.

This is the hardest moment—when the sun hits your eyes you are blind for a few moments, and have to wait for the eyes to adjust. You do that, standing stock still. It's not enough to just get reasonable vision, you wait until it is completely clear. That's good. Here we go.

With carefully measured strides, you walk forward. It's like a slow march—one step, pause, next step. Ten paces at one every second, and you arrive at the first body. No need to worry about the other three—your guardians will shoot if any of them moves. You keep your nose out of this as well. On the air is the dank smell of their rice—something about the way they cook it that is so distinctive—and that of lingering cordite, and gusts of the odour of excrement—one of them has shit themselves but who could blame them for that—and the sickly stench of exposed intestines that you remember as a boy when your father used to skin rabbits.

The young man. The one you went for. The weapon lies thrown clear. The M1—butt splintered by a bullet. Good, stand between man and weapon. You slide out your machete and bend, and the muzzle of the fuckin' SLR catches on the ground. Stupid fuckin' thing. But you don't want the M1 either. You just flick it with the machete down the track a way, out of reach. That'll be far enough.

Now, the man. He lies on his back and there are three huge holes in his chest—exit wounds coming through from his back. Good grouping. Check his hands—you can see both of them, his arms thrown wide. But he's fuckin' wrong way up!—think about that.

8

Maybe the impact sent him diving nose first into the ground, but he hit with such fuckin' force that he bounced over onto his back. Only explanation. He wouldn't have been alive long enough to roll himself. This was your target. You probably made a few of those holes. Somehow the image of the brilliant glowing tracers searing through the body is more awful. Check his eyes. You can see them, the rounded lids half-closed, vacant black pupils staring, and mouth gaping open—shouting a warning maybe that he never completed, carrying the final syllable away with him to eternity. No problem here. With those one per second strides, you walk around him and on to the second body.

The other young chap, lying half off the track, upper torso in the bushes. Makes it tough. Nasty leg wound, hidden by fabric but it bled excessively. Bleeding has stopped now. Good sign—for that much blood flow in so short a time it would have been spouting jets like a stream of piss when you continually squeeze your prick and interrupt the stream. Wouldn't mind a piss right now myself, or even a pull. The hard knob of your prick is rubbing on the fabric of your pants when you move, exquisitely irritating. Makes it fuckin' hard to keep your mind on the job. Yeah, so, you can see where the spray squirted to, a blood-puddle a yard from the wound, but now there's no heartbeat to pump it out. Good indicator, but not enough.

You'll have to move him. You look around but you can't see that fuckin' shotgun anywhere either. Might have thrown it way off into the bushes when he was hit. Might also have it under him, finger on the trigger, waiting to give you a little surprise when you roll him over. You go forward until you are standing with your toes right up against his hip, the SLR trained at the middle of his back. The slightest flicker of life and you'll fire.

This is very fuckin' dangerous, and very fuckin' awkward. You slip your left toecap under his hip, and raise him slightly. His empty left hand appears. Now you put the SLR in his earhole and reach down and grab a handful of his shirt under the armpit to hurl him over. But the fuckin' geometry is all wrong—length of your arms and SLR barrel, and for a vital terrifying moment, you are off balance, ill-prepared for whatever. Do it quick. Lift him and peep under-neath, ready to drop him again if necessary. You haul his upper torso off the ground for a moment. His arms fall limp. Good. No muscle resistance. You glimpsed that other hand and it was empty. No shot-gun, no hidden grenades. Okay to roll him, but you straighten first, get that muzzle levelled back at his head, and use your foot. Slip the toecap under his hip and flip him—over he goes. His head comes into view under the bush. His mouth is twisted remarkably, and then you see why—everything from his ear to his collarbone and corner of the mouth to the back of the neck is completely missing. Goner. Good. Can't see that fuckin' shotgun but...

"No weapon here, Nigel," you call—your voice astonishingly croaky.

"It's alright, Yogi. He threw it this way. We can see it. Keep going. You're doing fine."

Doing fine. Now the woman. She's right in the middle of the track, on her side, curled into the foetal position, her arms tucked in across her belly. No problem there. Her head has split open like an axe through watermelon and you can see the porridge of brainmatter splattered everywhere like dropped scrambled eggs. You move by her. The .303 is under her, still slung on her shoulder. She must have taken Mabel's burst full on—her middle part that she tried to de-fend with her arms is just a mincemeat mess. Her blouse has been torn right off her, and there is the delicate curve of a small breast. That doesn't help. You'll cream your daks in a minute if you don't keep your fuckin' fuckwit mind on the job. But you can still remem-ber what she looked like, in those fleeting moments before... Pretty woman, sweet smile, nice lithe body. Now a blob of offal. But even thoughts like that won't make that fuckin' erection go down. The pain is almost doubling you up, crippling now, your bladder and balls and intestines, all ready to burst. Get on with it, before you explode, like she did.

The man, father, leader. The weapon lies under him and so does one hand as he lies, face down. There's plenty of blood about him but no obvious wound. Stand still. You can feel what seems to be a scorpion clawing and scratching its way up your spinal cord, but that is only imagination. You want to be sick, to piss, to shit, to shoot your bolt. Bodily functions running riot. Watch him! Let it all flow but don't take your eyes off this fucker. There is, you are sure, the barest hint of movement. Perhaps a muscle flexing, a final reflex spasm, who knows. But movement. That's all you need. Without taking your eyes off him, you speak, very distinctly.

"This one's still kickin'."

Out of the void of silence, Nigel speaks. He is still back in there—covering you, watching your every move, but when he speaks it seems that he is right there, his lips at your ear.

"Finish it."

You don't need to move. From where you are there is a clear view of the back of the man's neck and the wet slicked black hair beyond. All you need. Your SLR remains at your hip, pointed downward and all you have to do is raise the muzzle a few inches, instincts tell you how far, and squeeze the trigger.

The abrupt single shot is deafening. You actually see the bullet hit, as if an invisible axe has crashed down on the man's neck and the entire body jolts, and when the skin jumps back to its proper place, there is a jagged hole, not round at all, and from the side of the head a brief geyser of blood shoots out. You watch with sullen fascination, until it stops.

"The rest are cactus."

"You sure?" Nigel asks.

"Yeah. Real brush and shovel jobs."

"Awright, you guys. Let's tidy this up."

Time to look to yourself. You step a few paces into the jungle on the far side of the track and unbutton your fly. There is a dark shiny stain all down the thigh of your greens—erk! Probably a few down the back as well. You try to piss but your bladder has nothing to offer, and the erection retracts even as you hold it. The bile had risen to your throat, but now it recedes. The crippling pain fades. All bullshit. Your body has been lying to you about what it wanted. Bloody stupid fuckin' thing. You button your fly and step back onto the track.

11

There is a lot of movement in the jungle behind you and the men of the section come through the foliage at various points and onto the track. Nigel, Snowy, Alby Dunshea, Bugsy, Sniffer and Greyman. They stand in a line, solemnly regarding their handiwork. Frozen in time and space. Their faces are lined with shock, with faint disgust, pale and drawn with strain. Nigel breaks the trance.

"You alright, Yogi?"

"Fuckin' marvellous."

"Awright. Bugsy, Alby—sentry posts right and left. Rest of you, get the gats and search the stiffs."

Bugsy and Dunshea move off to right and left. Nigel, you, Sniffer and Greyman will take one body each while Snowy, with Mabel cradled lovingly in his arms, stands protectively over you all like an old mother hen.

"Four kills, hey. And bodies to show for it," Snowy chortles with great pride—this is his best effort yet.

"Won't Hatrack be thrilled," Nigel says. "We'll be number one boys for this."

Greyman, eternally curious, prods at his body—the woman—with his bayonet.

"Hey, look at this! Her brains are gone and you can see right inside the skull."

Sniffer scurries over excitedly. "Yeah, mine's got an arm blown clean off. Aw, shit yeah. Get onto it. Like a passionfruit after yer've ate the guts."

"Awright, awright," Nigel is saying, though only because he must. "Cool the fucking biology lesson."

He stands away from his corpse, clutching the shotgun and going through some papers in a wallet he's found. You approach him, like Oliver Twist wanting more, only it is you with the offering. The weapon the father carried, a Russian AK47—now that you've wiped the blood and chunks of skin off the butt, is a real prize.

"This an AK47?"

You know it is.

"Yeah. Beautiful, aren't they. Better than our bloody shitsticks."

"Can I keep it?" you ask, almost pleadingly. "Give it a try?"

Nigel looks it over. It has the firepower of your SLR but it's half the length—a real advantage, for doing jobs like the one you've just done.

"Sure. If you can keep the ammo up to it," he says.

"No probs. Standard stuff, by the look of it."

You strip the magazine to show him. That magazine, so exotically curved, like a cruel piratic cutlass. Nigel nods his approval.

A prize. A real treasure. Something to show for it all when the story is told and retold back at Nui Dat. This the irrefutable souvenir of your finest moment. Excitedly you search the body for extra magazines and ammunition, and maybe best of all, the cleaning kit. And then Nigel is calling. "Awright, get yer shovels and let's get this lot under. Then let's go and see if we can find some more..."

2. Hoa Long

Just another of these shambled, thatched dwellings on yet another village search. This time it's Hoa Long—the closest village to Nui Dat but that doesn't make it any safer than any of the others. The troops go in at night, surround the town, close in at dawn and go methodically from house to house in section groups, searching, searching, fuckin' searching and finding fuck all. Except sometimes. Sometimes the inhabitants of the town are rounded up and gathered in a central location where Intelligence Officers examine identification papers and interrogate suspects while the men search the houses, going through all their belongings looking for weapons, unofficial documents, or large accumulations of food supplies. That's when they really think the Charlies are using the village at night. Other times, you just go in, bail up the people in their houses and have a bit of a look around. That's just a show of strength, to put the wind up 'em and discourage co-operation with Charlie. This one, this search of Hoa Long, is of the latter type.

"How many of these houses have you seen with a ceiling, Nigel?"

He doesn't answer you. He just looks upward and frowns. None is the answer. In the open-style living of your average Noggie, a ceiling can only be for hiding something.

There is a manhole up there, and Nigel circles on the floor, watching it carefully, eyeing it from every possible angle. The house is one room, but ten people live here—they are easy to count because you have them bailed up in the corner. One old man with traditional goatee beard, two old women with lips cherryroot red, a younger woman who might be the mother of the six children of varying ages and degrees of nakedness. The adults all wear the sheening black pyjamas. They all face one way, looking very concerned.

14

"What's up there?"

The gesture with the muzzle of your SLR makes the meaning plain, but they choose not to understand, and say nothing.

"Better have a look then," Nigel sighs.

You'd like to offer some sort of warning to the blokes outside, but you can't afford to take your eyes off this fuckin' lot. There's Spargo and Sniffer manning Mabel at the front of the house, Alby Dunshea and Bugsy to either side watching the back, Greyman searching the grounds. At moments like this, the manpower shortage is fuckin' critical.

Nigel begins to build a construction under the manhole. He drags the heavy table into place, heaves a smaller table on top, then a wooden trunk atop that. Looks pretty fuckin' rickety but it will have to do. The old man and young woman begin to murmur at each other and look very unhappy. Perhaps they are concerned that he will scuff the furniture, but that is unlikely. These bare floor houses are a mess anyway. Every morning the women sweep attentively the square in front of the house, but inside it's a rug on the bald earth and all their belongings piled upon it in utter chaos. It is impossible to tell where in here the ten people actually do their sleeping.

"You're being frowned at, Nigel," you say softly.

He starts making his way up toward the hatch. He leaves his Armalite on the tabletop and takes from a holster the Luger that is his own property. 'If we're gonna act like Nazis, we might as well look the part,' he commented on it previously, but it is jobs like this he was referring to. Now your hostages start muttering at each other with some urgency.

"Watch yourself, Nigel."

Nigel attains full height, lifts the hatch with the muzzle of the Luger, very slowly. He peeks over the edge but the opening faces the wrong way to allow a good view. Now he gives the hatch a heave and it flops over on the inside. He ducks, but nothing happens. Nigel raises himself and pokes his head up through into the ceiling...

Then ducks again...

There is a single shot!

Nigel comes toppling down, his whole rickety construction collapsing under him. The Noggies all scream and yell and dive for cover, as if they expect you are about to mow them down on the spot. Forget them—you're going sideways, one eye on that manhole, the other on the felled Nigel, who threshes about madly in a tangle of overturned furniture.

"He's going out through the roof!" Nigel roars.

Instincts take over. There are too many things to think about at once but you've stopped thinking anyway. It's all reflexes from here. Nigel's head is still attached to his shoulders—forget him. You've searched the house and there are no concealed weapons—forget the rest of the family. Nigel's problem anyway. There's a man on the roof—get him! That's all. You go charging like a wild animal, out of the house and into the sunlight.

Out there, people are everywhere. In these moments of action, time seems to slow down absurdly, while your mind races through everything you see, feel, sense. You glimpse Snowy on his feet, swinging Mabel around at the hip, the long trailing belt of ammunition flailing like a metallic snake. He's moving in slow motion, and he doesn't know where to look; staring at you with a quizzical expression. Wide of him, Sniffer on his knees, pointing his rifle all directions. In these confined jumbled places, a sound like a gunshot seems to come from everywhere at once.

"He's up on the fucking roof!" you scream wildly.

You can see him too. The afternoon sun throws the shadow of the house to the front and there a figure appears fleetingly, going left, jumping from the eaves into the alley at the side. You go that way, knowing full well that you are heading into Snowy's line of fire, but you also know that Snowy has seen you, knows where you are. Leading him onto the target, you bound to the front of the alley. The man, barechested, barefoot, black shorts, carrying what might be a .303. He's landed heavily, fallen, comes up on his feet, not knowing which way to run. Then he sees you, and bolts the other way.

Now there's the moment of crisis. You're in Snowy's line of fire and know it—either you get out of the way and give him a clear go at the

16

target or else you go after him yourself and risk getting a burst from Snowy up your bum.

"Yogi! Get outa the fucking way!" you hear Snowy roaring behind you, and you don't need to look—best not to anyway—to know he is on line down the alley. Just dive out of the way and leave him to it, all your instincts shriek. But no. There's other people moving up there!

One of them, you realise, is Dunshea who has moved in to block the other end of the alley—no shot for Snowy now. The target charges the astonished Dunshea and hits him full in the chest with a shirt-front any rugged half-back-flanker would be proud of; the shoulder right into the middle of the chest—whop!—and you actually hear the air expelled from Dunshea's lungs by the impact. He goes down flat on his back and the little man goes over the top and tumbles. Now you're the only opportunity and you race down the alley at full pace. The target comes up dazed, shaking his head, swinging that .303 wildly. He goes to take a pot shot to the right, toward Bugsy who must be over there somewhere, and then looks back and freezes when he sees you coming.

You roar like a charging elephant and the target's eyes widen as he sees you bearing down upon him. Three more strides and you'll have the little fucker by the throat and shake the fuckin' livin' daylights out of him, but you have to hurdle the fallen Dunshea, who is coming up dazed, your boot catches his shoulder and over you go—whacko!—flat on your face. The perfect bellywhacker on the hard ground.

When you glance up, the line-up is perfect. Straight between the target's legs you see Bugsy, down on one knee, his SLR at the shoulder—you're looking straight down the barrel and know how he's itching to have a go with it. The target quickly realises his good fortune. He probably can't believe the Griffin-Dunshea slapstick routine, much less that Bugsy hasn't cut him down yet. But Bugsy holds his fire and starts prancing sideways, going wide, fifteen metres away, looking for a line on the target that doesn't include you. By now Snowy and Mabel, and Sniffer and the pathetically hobbling Nigel

17

are coming down the alley. The little man is up and off, limping, running for his life, straight past Bugsy and toward the houses beyond.

You bounce and come up on your knees, swinging the AK around. You'll get him before he's made twenty yards and he needs thirty to any cover. You bring the butt to the shoulder, line him up, death narrows the gap...but no! Fuck it! *There's people back there.*

"Shoot him!" Nigel is roaring. "Splatter the little bastard!"

You're stumbling wide, lining up again, but always there are un-suspecting people beyond, standing, staring, and others moving about, still unaware of the drama. You realise now what Bugsy's problem was. Too many people. Innocent bystanders... You keep moving, searching for that clear line...too late.

By now the trampling herd has caught up and you join in. The target runs between two houses and you go after him, but when you emerge, you find you are in a wide marketplace, stalls all about the perimeter and a twenty yard clear circle in the middle. And about a hundred people, mostly women and children, all standing like an audience, wondering what street theatre they are watching.

The target has charged straight out into the middle and now darts this way and that, unsure of where to go. You come bowling through for another moment of confrontation, Snowy and Co. right on your heels.

"Get outa the way! Get outa the fucking way!" Snowy is bellowing and heaves the heavy gun to the shoulder. You get out of the way, but the target is running across the face of the crowd on the far side of the circle. Suddenly, they know the danger and a unified scream goes up.

It's only a moment but that's all it needs. Snowy, Sniffer, Nigel and myself, all with weapons aimed, twenty yards from the running man, easy shot. But behind him, frantic terrified people scatter. You'd get him all right but these high powered weapons don't stop at one body. A single shot from an SLR will go straight through him and five other people as well, the less controllable Mabel even in the mighty hands of Snowy will down a dozen or more.

Nigel throws his Armalite away and has the Luger out again—only 9mm single shot. Sniffer has abandoned his SLR and is after the man flailing his machete, but it is all too late. The target plunges through the wave of panicking onlookers, ploughing through screaming women shielding children hopelessly, others on the ground with their hands over their heads, still more running this way and that with their heads thrown back and the whites of their eyes and bared teeth showing. Too late. You run forward after Sniffer, but the target is gone, vanished, the chance lost.

Nigel is furious. He is redfaced with rage, bellowing at you all from a few feet away. "You let the fucker get away. He fuckin' near blew me head off and you let him get away!"

"Too many people," Snowy groans lamely. "We'd of wiped out half the fuckin' village!"

Nigel, in sheer frustration, looks about for someone else to blame, and finds the easiest target.

"What fuckin happened to you, Yogi? You had him, right here!"

You just give a hopeless shrug and let that be your answer.

But Bugsy can't be so sensible. "Calm down, Nigel. There's no fuckin' way we coulda got him."

"Try telling that to fuckin' Hatrack!" Nigel thunders.

It was right then that Greyman wandered onto the scene, his puzzled black face wondering what the commotion was all about.

"Where the fuck were you!" Nigel roars at him.

"I missed the whole thing," Greyman says cheekily. "Musta been fuckin' hilarious."

"But where the fuck were you!"

"I was having a shit, awright?"

"Yeah," Dunshea says laconically. "And so was everyone else."

Fifteen minutes later, the section is standing in a pathetic line in the middle of the village with the Noggies looking on and trying to pretend they don't know what's happening, and Hatrack, mood as black as thunder, laying into his men and all jutting angles—nose, ears, jaw, elbows, shoulders, hips. They call him Hatrack because of the way these bits stick out, perfect for hanging things on, except you think they meant *hat-stand*, but who cares. To them, the word Hatrack can be spat out in a way that says exactly what they feel.

"How the fuck did you all miss? It's wide open here!" he raged, and the Noggie audience all stepped back a pace to show how wide open it was. Hatrack was a most unreasonable man at any time, and all the more so when he was right.

"There were people, everywhere..." Nigel tried to tell him.

Hatrack stepped forward to hang the blame on individuals—it was his favourite technique.

"Come on, Snowy. You're the hottest M60 man in the outfit. Thirty, forty yards at most. How the fuck did you miss?"

"There was dust, people, sir," Snowy said lamely. "I never even saw him clearly. Closest thing I came to hitting was Bugsy."

Bugsy rolled his eyeballs with appreciation, but Hatrack wished only to offer him the slightest glance as he passed along the line. "Might have known you'd be in the way, Norris, as per fucking usual. What about you, Sniffer? Crack shot. What happened?"

"Like Nigel says, there was people everywhere. It woulda been a massacre, sir."

He arrived at Dunshea, who by then was sporting a splendid black eye from his collision. "Where'd you get that one, Dunshea?"

"I zigged on a zag, sir," Dunshea managed.

Hatrack, a man utterly devoid of a sense of humour, could never have grasped a concept like that.

"Billy the Greyman, away in the Dreamtime again were we?"

"I wish I was, sir."

You are at the end of the line.

"One of these days I'll wipe that silly grin off your face, Yogi Bear. Where were you? In hibernation?"

"No," you said softly. What you didn't say was `no, sir` but they had long since given up trying to get you to do that.

Truly, Hatrack could think of nothing further to say, and turned away, shaking his head in dismay.

"You owe me a body, Nigel. Make sure I get it."

We all wondered if his own might have filled the bill.

3. Perfect Timing

Tail-end Charlie again, bugger it all. Down the arse-end walking backwards, counting fucking paces for navigation. There's fuck all here anyway on this dead loss operation: Operation Broken Hill they call it—they name them all after towns in Aussie—and not a hill to be seen, broken or otherwise. Just this dead flat, scrubby jay in lightly forested country with occasional bamboo outcrops. No fucking Charlies either, fuck all. The company has propped for muckarm but there's this bit of a track and you get to go check it out. Just five hundred paces down, a listening post, in case the Charlies are coming. Fat fucking chance. Nothing's been along this track for years—the ground is soft and wet from the constant rain dripping from the forest canopy. No tracks. Why do they fucking bother?

Terry Gibson is forward scout, with Armalite and sawn-off shotgun slung and a couple of Claymore Mines in his pack, and a bloody poofta in most opinions but really loves machines better than people. You all reckon Greyman, being an Abo, oughta be scout but Nigel sticks with Gibson.

Nigel Naughton is next in line, a corporal many times busted, section commander, and a good bloke even if he's a whingeing Pom. Long and skinny with a huge waxed moustache, he has that sort of humour that keeps you going but gets you all the shit jobs when he turns it on the officers. He carries an American Armalite, a Luger on his belt, and the compass and map for navigation, every so often looking back to get the pace count from you, and then signalling the line of march forward to Gibson.

Next is Snowy Spargo, backcountry shearer and section gunner, yellow-haired of course. Snowy carries the M60 machine gun and bandoliers of ammunition slung Mexican bandit style off each shoulder, two more in his pouches, two more in his pack. Enough to stop a fair sized army. He's a fucking fanatic about that gun, calls her Mabel, mad jealous of inferring fingers, spends all his free time cleaning her, sleeps with her they reckon. For sure when he fondles her foresight or caresses her butt, you'd reckon there's weird stuff going down.

After Snowy comes his back-up—Bugsy Norris with his bent face and cow-eyed look, dumb Irish–Italian mongrel who signed on as a reg because being drafted allowed him to evade civilian changes for assault. He carries three belts of ammo for Mabel, a standard SLR for himself and carries slung the section M79 grenade launcher.

Then the Greyman, Billy Goolie, half-caste Aborigine, except he can't be because they aren't allowed to be drafted—a privilege reserved for Australian-born single white males. Trouble is, Billy looks like a full-blood Abo, and all the confusion that caused gave him his name. He likes to think his black half is free and roaming the Dreamtime, and hates his white half for getting drafted and dragging the rest of him into this mess. He carries a SLR and our M72 collapsible rocket launcher, and two more belts for Mabel, and he'd carry the radio if we had one but we don't. Won't need one on this short routine patrol, they reckon. They reckon...

Then Alby Dunshea, Section 2IC, big ugly prick and he hates everybody. He's one of them agros who need to beat up someone every so often to prove they exist, and you are just the sort he likes. Just because your big and not a fighter, or so he reckons. You can ignore him. It's just a pain in the fucking arse, that's all. Annoying, like scorpions. Dunshea is a lazy bastard and travels light, just an Owen Gun and a few grenades, to give anything he encounters a bit of a fright. With that twisted pockmarked puss of his, he'd give 'em a fright all right.

And Yogi Bear, down the back, covering their arses and checking the distance travelled.

You've come just one hundred and twenty-seven paces from the company perimeter when Gibson, who is half that distance again ahead of your position, reaches the apparent end of the track. Could be the shortest fucking patrol in history. There's this huge wall of thick bamboo, fifteen feet high and too dense for a fucking rabbit to squeeze through and it goes out of sight left and right. The track runs up to the wall and stops. Gibson stands, regarding the obstacle, looking like Ali Baba trying to remember the right words. Dead end, but if nothing goes any further, how come there's a track? Nigel gives him the signal to look around.

Down low he finds a hole. Maybe wild pigs made this track and forced an opening through the bamboo to the other side. Nigel nods and Gibson gets down on his knees and crawls through. It is like a tunnel in there, just big enough to fit a man on all fours but the bamboo has barbed runners that catch on everything and hurt like hell if you get one in you. It's only six feet to the other side but Gibson has to fight and jerk and thrust every inch of the way, muttering ceaseless curses under his breath. Then he emerges, and is unsure of his next move.

The rest of us are back on the other side of the wall, standing, waiting, but there's no reason to go through the hole if there's nothing on the other side. Gibson finds himself in a wide area of sparsely treed ground, flat and open and with a slight up-slope. Too flat, too open, but that doesn't click at first. He's looking for where the track goes next but there isn't any need for a track here—you can go any way you like. Ahead to the right there is a small clump of undergrowth and Gibson wanders that way, looking around, trying to make up his mind what to do. He's made over confident by reports that there are no Charlies within miles of this place. Safe ground. Routine check out.

Ahead, thirty yards away, he sees a mound of hard red earth, about two feet high. He looks at it and frowns. What could have made that? Then he realises there is another nearby, and another, maybe half a dozen in visual range all in a line... There's only one sort of creature could have made those mounds in so precise a geometric pattern... but Gibson doesn't realise that yet. But what he does get is a pungent odour on the air, sharp and distinctive, and when his nose detects that, then he gets the picture.

His next instinctive reaction saves his life. Instead of going back toward the hole to report or escape, he goes forward, leaping like a panther and hitting the deck beside that clump of undergrowth, rolling into the ditch out of which it had sprung. As he does, the five 30cal machine guns, one in each of the bunkers behind those mounds, open up. They blast their evil abrupt chatter, and worse is the whip-lash sound of the bright-sparked tracer-rounds as this torrent of gun-fire pours straight over the top of him...

... and straight at us on the other side of the bamboo wall. There's the frozen moment of horror as we realise we're in the shit, and then the instantaneous reaction—we scatter. Nigel and Snowy go to ground by the hole; Norris backs off the track and takes cover behind a fallen log and is out of the action; Greyman and Dunshea both dive for a ditch at the base of the bamboo and collide there—unknowingly they have placed themselves right in the line of fire from the bunkers to Gibson's position and will not be able to get their heads up.

A huge gap has opened up along the track between your position and that of Nigel and Snowy, fifty yards away. In your mind a single idea, impressed upon you in all those months of fucking training—if in doubt, go straight up the guts. And away you go, running flat out, from one side of the field of fire to the other. Halfway there, a long strand of barbed bamboo reaches down like a skeletal finger on the hand of God and plucks your hat clean off your head, and there it dangles, prancing like a puppet on a string—for a moment you think of dashing back to get it. It's the sort of shitwit thing that goes through your mind at a time like this. But you keep right on going and the hat dances in midair behind while you slide in like a baseball player, behind Nigel and Snowy, stripping off your pack, ready for action, almost entirely unaware that you have just done the most amazing thing of your life.

In fact your run across the field of fire isn't as brave as it seems. The downslope from the bunker position works against them and the silly fuckers are firing too high. The brilliant lizard tongues of tracers come shattering through the bamboo wall about ten feet up, showering you in a fog of dust and splinters. You're pinned down, but not in any immediate danger, but you don't realise that just yet. The downslope works for Gibson too, flat on his guts and digging-in with his finger and toe nails. They are ripping the foliage above him to shreds but they can't get him unless one of those gunners is prepared to expose himself and stand on tip-toe to get the downward angle required.

Which one of them might have done, had Gibson not started screaming. "Jesus, you blokes! It's fuckin' murder in here. Get me outa here! Get me fuckin' outa here!"

No one troubles to answer him, and he goes on yelling the same thing, over and over, but it does have two effects. It lets the others know he is still alive; and tells us exactly where he is. He is wide; to the right of the line from our position to what is to us the mysterious source of a hell of a lot of shooting. Which gives Snowy a go. He opens up with a long burst from the M60, shooting blind straight into the bamboo wall. His only concern is to miss Gibson, and that he does, until Mabel jams on him.

Snowy goes down on his knees, snapping the breech open in a fury and hurling the belt with the bent round aside savagely.

"Fuck fuck fuck fuck fuck..." he utters as he digs into the jammed shell casing with his razor-sharp bayonet. But his burst has worked—there won't be any Charlies standing on tip-toe to have a go at Gibson after that.

The Charlies are forced to revise their plan. Since they can't get the necessary down-elevation they launch a few grenades, while still keeping up the barrage of 30cal fire from their five gunposts to keep the attackers where they are. The grenades lob into the top of the bamboo wall and the tree canopy above and explode up there, four, five, six of them, like someone belting your eardrums with a hammer. Fragments of godknowswhat fly everywhere... But they're too high up, the rangefinding is bad, and then there's the dud that falls right beside Greyman.

The fire from the 30cals whiplashes overhead, the grenades erupt in the canopy. Gibson is screaming. "Jesus Christ, Nigel, get me outa here!" Snowy working on the breech of the M60. "...Fuck. Fuck. Fuck..." You are bellowing at Nigel. "Come on, Nigel. We gotta get him outa there!"

And in the middle of it all, from the platoon just back down the track, the plaintive voice of Lt Hollingsworth can somehow be clearly heard. "Do you need a medic up there?"

"Nar. Send shit paper!" Nigel retorts.

You have to laugh, you can't help it. Maybe it's some sort of hysteria arising from sheer panic, but you're on you knees, doubled up, giggling and burbling. And Snowy too bows his head over the jammed breech, his frenzied repairs abandoned to mirth. Nigel looks pretty pleased with himself. Gibson has heard it too, stops screaming for help and lies being steadily blanketed under a heap of leaves and branches, his face buried in his hands, chuckling madly. Back at company, they are all shaking their heads and guffawing away. Had the Viet Cong gunners been able to understand it, they probably would have been laughing too. He's like that, Nigel. Perfect comic timing.

Then the moment is gone and it's back to business. Gibson is screaming again. "Will ya stop cracking fuckin' jokes and get me fuckin' outa here! It's fuckin' murder in here!"

"Come on, Nigel," you are yelling. "We gotta get him out!"

Naughton knows it. "Okay, you guys, come on! Let's go! Straight up the guts!"

Snowy is still frantically prising at the jammed shell, with his bayonet, and he digs it out, slaps in the new belt, slams down the breech...but it all takes too long. You've launched your way forward and you go right past him and down on all fours into the hole. You scramble madly, barbs tear your shirt and your skin but you pay it no heed, grunting like the wild pig that made this hole, clawing your way through. You hear Snowy behind you, dragging the gun, growling like a tiger, and the others are coming too now, Greyman has barrelled out of the box he was in with a tribal roar and Dunshea is right with him, and Bugsy too—heads down, showered by splinters from the ongoing barrage, all queuing behind Nigel to get into that hole.

You come up on the other side, the open ground, get on your knees and start firing wildly until Snowy is there beside you, and opens up with Mabel. That'll keep 'em down, and you go. You're guided by Gibson's continued screaming, running flat out across the ground, pumping off the remaining rounds in your mag as you go. You hit the deck rolling, tumble again, and come up beside Gibson who is almost completely buried in a carpet of shattered leaves and branches.

"G'day, Gibbo. Havin' a bit of trouble?"

He looks at you blankly, and then pure joy spreads over his freckled and mud-splattered face. Plainly he's never been so happy to see anyone in his entire life.

"Jesus, Yogi. What took yer so fuckin' long?"

The rest of them are through and deploying, but you realise the incoming fire has stopped. They've gone. They've seen you giving them the fuckin' charge and reckoned there must be hundreds of you, instead of just this six man patrol, and they've pissed off quicksmart. Nigel rushes one of the bunkers and lobs in a grenade, and then another and does it again, but there is no longer anyone at home.

"Okay, you guys, cool it," Nigel says. "Stay where you are."

And he looks at you. "How far did we come?"

"Hundred and twenty-seven paces," you somehow miraculously remember. What silly things brains are!

Nigel grins and turns to the others. "Alby, go back and guide the platoon into here. Rest of you, spread out and hold ground."

You lie beside Gibson, a man at the bottom of a compost heap.

"Jesus, look at this place," he says grimly.

Everything, trees, bushes, bamboo, is shorn off at a height of about three feet. The wood is completely splintered and the whole lot dumped on Gibson—like a kid's game in the heaps of autumn leaves. Next day the newspapers back in Aussie will have his picture and tell how he was trapped under a tree trunk that fell on him—all bullshit as newspaper accounts usually are. There's nothing left of this mess that anyone would call a tree trunk—it's just a tangle of mangled and splintered foliage. You haul him out. Both of you are a little weak at the knees.

The rest of the platoon comes up, men hack the bamboo wall to increase the size of the hole, and they pass by you and the bunkers and check the place out. The platoon commander, Holly, is amazed by what he sees. He calls up the Company. He calls down airstrikes and artillery on the far side of the camp. The Company arrives, and Hatrack is all the more astonished, and calls in the Battalion, Engineers, Intelligence and more airstrikes.

The reports come back. The camp is huge—large enough to harbour a thousand people. They are finding caches of food and weapons, documents and equipment. It seems they were all at home when Naughton's section hit them and went running out the other side of the camp; men, women and children, fleeing into the jungle where now the Phantoms and B-52s are pounding the living daylights out of them. Poor bastards. Five or so men stayed behind to man the 30cals and keep the attackers at bay until they got clear. They were never really trying to hit anyone, they were just trying to slow us down. There were no blood trails—nobody got hurt. There were no officers present—nobody got any medals.

Months later the ARVN found a mass grave in the area beyond the camp, presumed to hold the victims of the airstrikes that befell them as they fled the camp that day. There were conflicting reports as to the number of bodies—between fifty and two hundred and fifty. No one confirmed it. No one bothered to try. It was already ancient history. In the grave there were women and children and well as men—nobody knew what to think about that and so didn't think anything.

You'll never to do anything half so brave again, if brave was what it was. They left your hat dangling from that overhanging bamboo runner as a sort of shrine to what took place that day—maybe its still there. It's not the sort of place people go to often. That was why the camp probably thought itself safe.

An hour later you and the others sat leaning on a tree trunk, still shaking, soaked in sweat, smoking. It was the fifth cigarette of your life, all of them lit of the end of the previous one. Terry Gibson came by and grinned at Billy Goolie. "Hey Greyman," he calls. "If you want the forward scout job from now on, it's yours."

"No thanks, mate. Somehow I seem to have gone right off the idea. You're better than me anyway."

It really hurts Greyman to say it, but he's gotta, and that's that.

"Better at leading us into trouble, maybe," Gibson laughs.

Nigel sees the need to pass judgement. "But you knew they were there, Gibbo. That's what matters."

"Yeah," Gibson says, headbowed with a humility that probably isn't false. "It was when I smelled 'em. That's when I knew."

Nigel laughs. "Then it's your nose I want up front, so you can keep on sniffin' 'em out for us."

Maybe it was a massacre, maybe it was a great victory, maybe it was a trivial skirmish in which no one got hurt. No one could ever tell. There's a painting purporting to depict *The Broken Hill Contact* in the Canberra War Museum, but really it doesn't give too clear an impression of what happened. Books on Australia's involvement in Vietnam see no reason to mention the incident; there was no bodycount so nobody cared. For us the only tangible evidence that it ever happened was that thereafter Terry Gibson was renamed *Sniffer*, and the only part of the whole damned thing to make its way into military history was Nigel Naughton's immortal joke.

"Do you need a medic up there?"

"Nar. Send shit paper!"

4. Buddha's Day Off

An old man lay dying on a low narrow cot in a musky darkened room. You knew he was dying the moment you parted the long veil hanging over the doorway and peered into the dim interior. You can smell it when people are dying like this—a particular odour of human decay that permeates these places, these so-called villages where so-called people lived. Human beings they might have been by species, but the RSPCA would not allow animals to live the way these people do, or have to. In this damp tropical heat everything rots immediately, and what these people—these villagers—possess; their houses, their belongings, their children, their lives, all reek of active decomposition. The odours of rotting things fill the land, reaching into even the remotest parts of the jungle—it turns your stomach until you get used to it, and then you, like them, don't care anymore. But the smell of rotting human flesh is different to all the other rotting smells, different even to that of decomposition after death. As soon as you parted the curtain, and even before your eyes became accustomed to the darkness, and you could make out only the vague form of the cot, you told yourself: a man lies there and he is dying.

You slipped the safety on your AK47 and raised the muzzle carefully until it pointed at the figure—you could make all the assumptions you liked on the basis of the best possible knowledge, but that didn't mean you could be careless. You made no movement, waiting for your eyes to adjust to the dimness, to sharpen their focus. A dying man hidden in a darkened room might well be Charlie, having crawled here in his agony to await a sad, ignominious death in the stifling darkness. Such a dying man might see you as a last chance at glory, attained by a pistol or hand grenade hidden under the pillow. You waited, until you could be sure. There were no chances left worth taking.

Slowly, too slowly, your eyes began to make him out. Both hands were visible, one draped across his belly, the other dangling off the edge of the cot, almost touching the floor. Skeletal, withered hands. But he was clear. You looked quickly about the room for hiding places in case he had friends, but it was solid brick, three paces wide, seven long, with no cupboards or alcoves, nowhere to hide. There was only you and the old man—you slipped the safety and lowered the AK and quietly paced to the side of the cot.

He was old, very old and thin, an emaciated torso threaded through a loincloth, with the sash of a bandage on his gaunt, prominent ribs. His head lolled over the end of the cot—he wasn't seeing you, or anything. His stomach moved slightly with his faint breathing, eyes open and gazing at a precise point on the ceiling. He was so thin that his ribs stood out like curved pickets on a fence, and the bandage, six inches wide and wrapped right around his body, bulged where cotton wool had been stuffed in on the right side of his ribcage; got him clean through the lung, you reckoned. The old man's eyes wobbled around to look at you for a moment, his head lifting slightly from the mattress, and although he saw you, no expression registered on his face. Then his head fell back, teeth bared, nostrils flaring in his struggle to breathe.

He was an old man like so many old men in these villages, needed now to do the work because there were no young men. In these villages all the young men and young women had been drafted into one army or the other, or were dead, and old men like these were the strength of the community, with their big smiles and goatee beards, offering the soldiers rice wine, squatting in clusters and nodding knowingly. The children ran about in the mud and squalor between the shanty buildings, splattered with the slime of the streets, crowding about the soldiers begging for Salem—they preferred mentholated fags—and chop-chop—food of any kind. In return they offered their sisters, who were all under thirteen or else really their mothers and over forty. The 'sisters' in question stood tittering in doorways and looked as nubile and enticing as they could. And the old men squatted, nodding their wisdom, paying no heed. In a world ridden with poverty, there was no generation gap. The old men squatted with their bare feet in the shit, sucking their cherryroot pipes, watching the soldiers go by as they had all their long lives.

This old man was a priest, you assumed, for the room was in a temple. One of those shaven-headed Buddhist priests in bright orange robes who sat in city squares and doused themselves in petrol and went up in a ball of flame. No one really understood why they did that. No fiery death for this old bugger though—just this scungy mattress on a sagging cot.

There was a robe, white not orange, by the bed. You leaned the AK on the cot and picked it up and rolled it into a ball and placed it under his bald cranium. The flesh was clammy to touch, repulsive, but at least that allowed his mouth to close, sparing you his rotten teeth, black where they weren't yellow. Now you reached for the bandage, to see what you could see, and saw his eyes widen with horror, but you needed to examine that wound. You raised the cotton wool a few inches and promptly let go again as a pungent smell of gas gangrene gushed up at you nauseatingly:

"Jesus."

There was a hole under there all right and it was huge—how huge you didn't need to know. The old man gazed at you with his expressionless expression. You sighed, picked up the AK and pushed through the thin woven veil back to where the brighter light of the temple interior savaged your eyes.

It was a Buddhist temple—the squatting gentleman, surprisingly thin in effigy, occupied that space where altar and cross would have been in what you had experienced as a church. There were no pews—the faithful knelt directly on the mosaic stone floor—wobbly knees like yours would have been tested here. It was a massive stone building, of French influence, layered with pink plaster that was riddled with bullet holes and chunks exploded away. It was the largest building in the town except for the Catholic Church. But that was why you were here, wasn't it.

In this main interior of the temple, Greyman drifted, his heritage baffled by the symbols and effigies and artefacts of devotion that, to atheistic you, was the same nonsense in different clothes.

"Hey Billy. Go get Nigel, quick."

Greyman turned quietly and with all due reverence made his way outside. You looked back toward the veil, but there was no reason to return in there. Because it seemed the natural way to go, you walked slowly toward the Buddha, squatting upon a pedestal more than a man's height above the level of the room. An angelic ray of sunlight reached down to touch the exulted face, and your eye traced it upward. There, high on the gables, was a hole—three or four tiles were missing, the terracotta fragments scattered on the floor. Following that line led you to the step at the foot of the Buddha where there was a patch of dried blood. Someone should have cleaned up by now, you would have thought.

Yesterday Charlie rocketed a convoy of trucks just outside this village and brought an airstrike of Phantoms down upon themselves. Those big 50 cal shells could bounce and go for miles and still hit with sufficient force to turn those roof-tiles into shrapnel. That was the answer, for sure. The poor old bugger was still probably wondering how he had provoked the Buddha to strike him down so savagely.

"Whatever he said, he didn't mean it," you remarked to Buddha's fat-lipped smile.

That attack had brought you here—too late since any Charlies worth catching would have been long gone, but orders were orders. Hatrack's men descended upon the village and went from house to house, searching through everything, checking everyone. It was all to demonstrate that the Uc Dai Loi did not take lightly their men and equipment being mistreated so.

"Uc Dai Loi Number One. Vit Cong Number Ten," the Noggies told you incessantly. It was harder to believe every time you heard it.

This was a village under constant pressure from Charlie and the

33

search was thorough and complex in its planning. Near Nui Dat the Sappers were building a complete town surrounded by barbed wire, and many of these people would be rehoused there where they could be guarded or protected, out of Charlies' reach, and forcibly moved if necessary. Intelligence officers would come and interview or interrogate all families, and your job was to clear the way for them, to ensure they got no nasty surprises.

A temporary hospital had been set up in the marketplace, offering medical attention in return for 'hearts and minds'. There they were to dispatch any sick or injured people, but already the unexpected proportions of that task was overwhelming them. Everywhere they went there were people with missing limbs or foul sores, children bloated with malnutrition, women with hideous skin infections, old men so deformed that their hands touched the ground when they walked. Disease dominated this place; it was as if the town itself was a festering wound. Even most of their mangy dogs were three-legged. Ten Platoon found two young men with gangrenous legs turned black and as thick as their bodies—undoubtedly Charlies too ill to escape the cordon. But there were also many wounds on women and children, caught in the crossfire. Every one of them had to be escorted or carried to the Medical Area, and this old man just another.

The plod of Nigel's rubbersoled boots resounded in the chamber of the temple as he came in, tailed by Greyman.

"What's the go, Yogi?"

You jerked a thumb toward the room with its cobweb veil and Nigel strode on in without hesitating and came right out again.

"Holy fucking mother of Siddhartha. What a fuckin' pong!"

Obviously he had not had time to examine the wound.

"Copped a ripper." Your voice reverberating across to him from where you stood on the steps. "Right through the lung. Looks like a 50 cal. Come in up there and zapped him while he prayed to the enlightened one."

"The bolt from the blue, hey? If he was Catholic, they'd make him a saint for this."

You smiled, but Nigel looked about bleakly, helpless and hesitating—these sorts of days were the worst of all. The natural environment of the Uc Dai Loi was the jungle—you felt awkward and vulnerable in these urban situations.

"Billy," he said finally. "Go down to the Medical Area and bring back a doctor."

Greyman, who had also gone in for a gander and been driven out by the stink as swiftly as Nigel had, did not respond. You knew why, and looked firmly at Nigel.

"He's fucked," you said.

"I know that! But we can't just leave him there."

"Why not? He's probably supposed to die in there. Part of their religious mumbo-jumbo. Why not just leave him to it?"

"If you wanted to do that, Yogi Bear, you wouldn't have called me in," Nigel said slyly.

"I just thought you might be interested."

Nigel didn't answer, turning to Greyman. The buck passed.

"Go get the quack, mate. Take Sniffer with you for backup."

Greyman nodded sadly and went off. You followed.

"I need you here, Griffin," Nigel said fiercely.

"I'm just going outside for some fresh air," you said.

Wisely, Nigel let that happen.

You stepped through the columned portals of the temple where once great doors had hung—the rusted hinges were still there, the bolts still clinging to fragments of shattered timber. Walking forward on the stone forecourt chipped and scarred by explosions and bullets, you stopped one pace short of where the line of shade ended and the dazzling area exposed to the sun began. The Temple had a high wall around it, topped by shattered glass—the poor man's barbed wire—and a broad area of carefully swept dirt lay between the building and the wall. In front of every building in every town in Vietnam the ground was swept every morning, and the bare dirt surface rendered smooth as concrete. The footprints of the soldiers showed clearly here. No one else, you could see, had done any walking that morning.

Snowy had set up Mabel over by the wide gateway in the wall, facing outward through the opening toward the village. He and Bugsy made use of the shade of a huge tree that grew outside but extended branches over the wall. Snowy was brewing coffee, but Bugsy was facing back into the courtyard, rifle across his thighs as he sat propped against the wall, and when he saw you he motioned toward the area to the right of the building. You nodded, and, keeping in the shade, moved along the raised forecourt in that direction.

Inside the compound were several other buildings; those to the left of the temple seemed to be a school of some kind, and behind that was a barn or storehouse, to the right and behind the temple was what might have been a low prison cell block, most likely the quarters of the monks. They had split their forces—yourself and Greyman into the temple proper; Nigel and Sniffer down to check out the school and barn; Dunshea on his own but covered by Snowy and Bugsy, to search the quarters. This last stage of the plan had not worked out, you saw as you reached the right side of the temple. About thirty monks with their orange robes, bare feet and shaven heads, were standing in a line outside their quarters, murmuring to each other and looking very unhappy and each carrying a tall wooden staff. Dunshea stood before them, wondering what to do next.

"Hey, Alby, what's up."

He looked around edgily; plainly he did not want to turn his back on his tormentors.

"They won't let me in."

"Maybe you didn't ask politely enough."

Dunshea snorted through his thick nose and backed up until he was level with you, never taking his eyes off the gathering. Maybe it was his great ugly puss that was bothering them, but you missed the chance to say so.

"Where's Nigel?" he asked.

"Inside. We got a sickie."

He nodded, keeping his eyes on those monks. So did you. They didn't look any happier now that their antagonist had moved away. There was about forty yards between them and you now.

"These blokes won't let me in," Dunshea explained. "Being right nasty about it."

"Probably because of your winning smile," you offered. "Nigel know about them,"

"Yeah. He saw them."

"They probably think we're invading sacred ground or something," you proposed, though you really didn't know anything about it. "Keep an eye on them."

"I'll keep both eyes on them, I'll give 'em somethin' to chant about."

You nodded. He sat on a parapet in the shade of the temple, facing that unmoving line of orange.

"Better not let them get hold of any petrol drums," you added and immediately regretted it; the images accompanying that remark were better not conjured.

"Piss orf yer iggle-headed pooftas," Dunshea growled. "Yer give me the creeps."

You walked slowly back toward the temple entrance, but paused when Snowy signalled from the gate. Moments later, Greyman and Sniffer came through, followed by Ten Days, who as medic might prove useful, and Lt Hollingsworth, who certainly wouldn't. All four pulled up short when they saw the gathering of monks.

"What's with these chaps?" Holly wanted to know.

"Fan club," Dunshea said dryly. "We seem to have lost their hearts and minds."

Holly gave Dunshea the bleakest of looks, and then, because officers have to give orders now and then to prove to themselves that they are officers, he turned on Snowy. "Why haven't you turned the gun around, Private Spargo, to face the threat from these hostiles?"

"Buddhist monks are pacifists, sir. They aren't allowed to be hostile."

"They don't look in a pacifistic mood to me, Private Spargo," Holly determined.

"Maybe it's their day off," Greyman mused.

We all chuckled until Holly, reddened with fury, snapped his final word. "Turn the gun around and watch them, Private Spargo. This is a war zone. No such thing as a pacifist here."

You turned, shaking your head, to lead them into the temple, knowing that Snowy would leave Mabel exactly where she was.

The cooler air inside was a relief after the unbreathable rancid stuff out there—still Sniffer and Greyman saw the sense in not following and took up places near Dunshea. It was always wise to keep out of the sight and mind of officers, even harmless ones like Holly.

Nigel sat on the steps below the Buddha, brewing a mug of tea right there on the floor of the holy chamber.

"I thought I asked for a doctor," he said, eyeing Ten Days with disdain.

"The doctors have their hands full at the Medical Area," Ten Days explained. "House calls just aren't on."

Holly had vertical lines to either side of his mouth that worked like fish gills when he was irritated.

"What have you got for us, Nigel?"

Nigel looked at you.

"Old man with a six inch hole punched through his ribs," you pointed in all the appropriate directions. "Looks like a 50 cal came in through the roof and got him while he prayed to the big fella."

"A sign from Nirvana, I imagine," Holly remarked. Only the eternal smile of Buddha could endure the same joke for a third time. But God, in any religion, was definitely not an American pilot.

Ten Days went in through the veil and Holly followed, took one gasping breath, and came right out again. To justify that little embarrassment, he turned sharply on Nigel. "So what are you doing about the situation outside?"

"What situation outside?" Nigel asked, stirring his tea assiduously.

"The monks seem to be agitated by our presence here."

"And rightly so," Nigel said. "Yeah, I saw them as I came in. They won't bother us if we don't bother them."

"They look in a fairly dangerous mood to me."

"Not half as dangerous as I bet we look to them."

"I did not come here for a philosophical discussion, Corporal Naughton."

Neither Nigel nor you bothered to ask why he had come, making

38

his superfluous presence all the more evident.

Ten Days saved what might have been a regrettable confrontation by reappearing through the veil. The fierce gust of pungent air that came with him said that the bandage had been changed. Fat lot of good that was.

"He's rooted," Ten Days pronounced solemnly. "Buggered if I know how he's still alive."

"We already know that, clown," Nigel bit at him, wearying now.

The tirelessly formal Holly said, "What do you suggest, Corporal Hollis?"

"We'll have to take him to the interrogation area, I guess," Ten Days proposed with a helpless shrug.

Nigel was shaking his head. "I suspect our friends outside mightn't like that. That's why I wanted the doctor brought here..."

Holly bristled. Ten Days continued to tread the tightrope between them. "Prob'ly nothing the doc could do even if he did come."

"So what's the point of taking him down there?" Nigel seethed.

"Well I don't know," flustered Ten Days.

But Holly did. "Orders state specifically that all ill and injured are to be removed to the Medical Area for treatment. The major was quite adamant about that."

"Fuck Hatrack!" Nigel bellowed.

And we were all happy to allow that to echo about the chamber for a few moments.

Throughout all this you had shown the good sense to keep your thoughts to yourself, but now Nigel had negated himself with anger and Ten Days with confirmation of the obvious.

"Why don't we just leave him here to die in peace," you suggested, as if you'd just thought of it.

"We can't do that," Holly said. "It's inhumane."

"So's moving him," you countered. "Even if we get past the orange hordes outside, he probably won't survive the trip."

"If we get him down there," Ten Days put in. "They might be able to give him something to ease his pain...or...something."

"He's not in any pain," you debated. "They have this meditation stuff that causes them not to feel a thing."

"What would you know about it, Private Griffin?" Holly interjected.

He was right. You had no particular knowledge of such matters, but you didn't need to know much to work this out.

"Obviously he is supposed to die in there, right where he is."

Holly glared at you angrily. "Well what do you want to do, Yogi Bear? Go in there and belt him over the head and finish him off?"

You looked at Nigel. For both of you that seemed a remarkably sensible suggestion.

But it had developed into one of those situations where Holly could see that all this arguing was eroding his sense of authority and self-importance. You were merely a diversionary tactic, and now he turned on Nigel and made his stand as fiercely as so small a man could manage.

"You will move him, Corporal Naughton, to the Medical Area, and that is an order. If you don't have him down there in half an hour, it'll be your stripes, and I mean it. I'm going to round up some more men in case those chaps outside decide to make trouble. But you get him down there, and do it now."

He turned on his heel and marched away, getting out before anyone could raise further dispute. You slept better, knowing that your leaders were strong and wise.

Nigel, still seated on the steps, dashed the dregs of his tea at the feet of the Buddha.

"Alright Ten Days, how do we go about this. Pick him up, bunk and all..."

Ten Days was pained by the need to think about it. "No. Too bumpy and awkward. Best if you just pick him up in your arms and carry him that way."

Nigel looked at you from under his heavy brow. "You found him, Yogi. He's yours."

You didn't want to be looked at, though it was fair enough. You had, after all, started all this. Nigel continued looking, and finally you handed your AK to Ten Days. Still, you could manage one final attempt at sanity.

"Aren't we gonna wait till Holly brings the extra men?"

"Fuck Holly!" Nigel roared. Somehow, his name did not resound half as much as Hatrack's did.

You returned to that abysmal room. The old man lay as before, unmoved by all this moralising on his behalf. Nigel and Ten Days took up position to either side, to render what assistance they could, but they weren't needed. You slipped one arm under the old man's shoulders, the other under his thighs and started to raise him.

"Shit, he doesn't weigh anything," you breathed.

The expressionless expression and bulging eyes fixed on your face, but there was neither resistance nor cooperation. You cradled him against your chest as best you could, then turned and headed out into the temple proper.

"When you get outside, head straight for the gate, pronto, no matter what," Nigel yelled urgently, and darted ahead of you while Ten Days scurried along behind.

You carried him easily, maintaining a balanced brisk stride without jolting him around too much, and so you proceeded out of the temple and into the sunlight.

Nigel went bolting across the courtyard ahead of you. "Snowy! Grab the gun, get behind Griffin, cover him. Rest of you, form a line, here, right now."

Given its unexpectedness, the response was like lightning. As you came out with your pathetic burden and the fussing Ten Days at your heel, Snowy was already running into position with the bulky Mabel, and Nigel was hastily gathering the others into a line facing the monks, blocking their access to the gate. Immediately a cry went up from the monks, and you glanced over your shoulder to see them running forward in a tight bunch, awkward in those orange robes, waving their staves over their heads.

"Keep going Griffin, whatever happens," Nigel was yelling above the din. "Awright, you guys. Back up, real slow, and for fuck's sake don't shoot anybody."

You had about thirty yards to make across the courtyard to the gate, Ten Days running ahead now, Snowy walking backwards be-

hind you. The monks broke their run just short of the line of soldiers, and they levelled weapons at each other, the men with guns
backing off, those with staves coming on menacingly. Nigel and his
band were brandishing their rifles and shouting abusive threats at
their adversaries, while the monks jabbed at them with the staves,
uttering angry chants and fearful cries.

You reached the gate and glanced back—the converging forces
were just twenty yards away and closing. Then one monk lashed
savagely at Nigel with his stave. Nigel parried the blow easily, swiftly
reversed his Armalite and, stepping a pace against the traffic, brought
the butt down firmly on the monk's shining dome. The plastic butt
of the Armalite cracked from one end to the other, and the monk
took a nosedive into the dirt.

Everything stopped then. And you had stopped too, right at the
gateway, realising that there was no reason to go any further. At precisely the same instant Nigel struck the monk down, the old man in
your arms jolted violently, as if the blow had struck him. The convulsion was so sudden that you almost dropped him, and then you
immediately wished you had.

The soldiers, frozen in various combat postures, realised that something had happened, and turned toward you as you turned toward
them. Blood had exploded out of the old man's every orifice, gushing from nose, mouth and earholes and gurgling out from within his
bandage and loincloth to splatter in a ghastly puddle at your feet,
splashing onto your boots. You just stood in horror and repugnance,
the old man dangling lifelessly in your arms.

Staves and rifles were lowered. The monks halted their advance
and gathered about their felled comrade, and Nigel and his men
turned and walked to join you at the gate. The monks did not give
chase. They helped the dazed man to his feet, murmuring to themselves, not even looking the way the soldiers had gone.

The men of four section gathered around you, and most had to
turn their backs.

"Well, that's it," Ten Days pronounced unnecessarily.

Nigel bowed his head and then looked back to where the monks had gathered. Then he hurled his cracked weapon across to Dunshea who caught it deftly. "Give him to me," he said solemnly.

You were thankful to obey.

Slowly, reverently, Nigel carried the old man back toward the monks, walking right up to them and lowering the body to the ground at their feet. Any one of them could have belted him over the head, had they wanted. Nigel straightened, paused as if he intended to say something to them but did not, and then turned and came back toward the gate.

He went straight by you, snatching his weapon from Dunshea's hands as he passed. The others sullenly followed along. Behind, the monks fell upon the ground and began to wail for the lost soul of their dead companion. You wiped the blood from your hands on your greens, took your AK back from Ten Days, and followed after Nigel.

5. Riders on the Storm

Fading in again... remember the rain beating down directly on your face, torrential rain sharply pummelling your cold flesh. Seems strange to be lying there like that, flat on the back, face upturned into the rain, making no attempt to defend yourself from it; you can feel it running in tiny rivulets—across the hollows of the eyes, down between the nose and cheeks, splashing over the lips... open those lips slightly to take some in... nice, cool, refreshing... Yet you feel so cold... got to open the eyes and see what's happening, but the rain pounding the eyelids won't allow it... can't do it... raise a hand to shield them and try... that's better... You open the eyes slowly but they immediately fill with the water... close and squeeze to get rid of it then open again... it's still a watery blur and even when that clears there is only blackness... the back of your hand barely distinguishable from the dark wet world beyond... Rain pouring down and you can hear the wind howling out there... but it's all blackness and then intermittent flashes of blinding light that are only momentary whiteness... Nothing can be seen... there is no anchor for your senses... just the storm... oh yeah, you remember the storm. The storm rages in the night and is no dream, no nightmare, or else the nightmare is real. You remember the storm.

Nigel warned you about the storm. A typhoon no less, brewing out in the South China Sea, heading toward the coast of Vietnam. Not this far south though. Way up north. Ho in Hanoi, they'd really be copping it. Still its effects even at this distance were powerful enough...

You saw it coming as you flew in the chopper, one of a row of a dozen in two files, flying across the face of a massive brooding cloud formation in the shape of a giant anvil that filled the sky in that direction—the advance forces of the raging monster behind. You watched it closing in with sullen silent faces, the sunlit billows atop ranging downward through deepening shades of increasingly troubled grey to the dismal streaky downpour on the jungle beneath. Even in the chopper you could feel the new sharpness, the chill, on the wind. In all these months of heat you had forgotten cold, but that didn't mean you sweated any less. You sat in the rattling chopper taciturnly observing the approaching cold front, silently cursing it as one more hardship to overcome.

You sat on the lurching metal floor with feet dangling over the side, along with Snowy who clutched his beloved Mabel to his chest and Nigel, both watching the storm as you did, teeth gritted in disgust. Out there the other choppers, flying westward over the central mountains to the flatter country in the fartherest reaches of the province. No Man's Land. The choppers slid up and down like pistons in an engine, shaken constantly by variable turbulence, dropping into sudden air pockets, the rotors flapping frantically for purchase in the gusting air, quivering with vibration, twisted continually from their relentless course by the irrational wind.

At the head of the line, the two gunships peeled off and banked toward a distant clearing and went racing back and forth while you circled, waiting, at two thousand feet. The gunships skipped about the clearing at treetop height, guns blazing into the forest on both sides, until they decided it was clear and one dropped a red smoke grenade, and then your choppers banked around and began the descent, shuffling into single file, anxiously bouncing and thumping their way toward the earth. And all the time the gunships zipping back and forth, holding the ground.

"They say there's a camp at this place called Ap An Quai and the SAS reckon its brim full of Charlies," Nigel had said. "We're going in to clean the fuckin' joint out."

"Oh sure," Snowy answered in flat monotone. "I reckon we'll be sweepin' the gutters and pickin' up the garbage. There hasn't been a Charlie within miles of one of these camps yet."

"Be that as it may," Nigel said, not smiling at all as he sipped from his mug of tea. "Our wondrous leader Hatrack has decided we haven't earned our pay this week, so in we go to have a geek."

He jabbed an indicatory finger at the flat green continuum of the map he had laid out on the ground before you. "We fly in to this point here and then march five thousand metres to this Ap An Quai place. That's it there."

"Five thousand metres!" Greyman cried. "Shit, what do we do after breakfast?"

Nigel smiled flickeringly now: "We have breakfast first, but we are in a hurry. We want to get in and out by nightfall. There's a big storm on the way and they reckon it might turn into a typhoon by tonight. We have to get there, check the camp out, and get back to Nui Dat before it hits."

"Nice to have an easy day for a change," Sniffer said dully.

...yes, it is night and the storm has hit with all the expected force, but you never got back again... You were still here, in the camp, in the storm, in the rain, lying flat on your back and helpless.

"Is someone there?"

"Yeah, Yogi. I'm here, mate."

A dark shape looms over you, a blacker area amid the general black-ness. Lightning flashed and you can see it is the head of a man with a soggy fag dangling from his lips and a voice that itself is low and grumbling, like the storm. Knew him...

"That you, Bugsy?"

"Who else?" he chuckles. "How you feeling, Yogi?"

"Pretty fucking shithouse."

"Any pain?"

"Nar. Didn't bring your umbrella, did you?"

"Sorry, Yogi. There just isn't any place out of the rain around here."

"Guess we didn't make it back to The Dat, huh?"

"Not even nearly. You'll be there soon though. The choppers are on the way to take you sickies out. Us poor healthy bastards will have to stay out here all night."

"Tough titty. I wish they'd fuckin' hurry."

You seemed to have been lying there forever, for all your known life.

"Lucky to get them out in this," Bugsy ruminates. "All aircraft are grounded but a bunch of RAAF cowboys said fuck that! Pinched their own choppers to run the dust-offs in unflyable conditions. They can probably only do it because they'd all be pissed to the eyeballs at this hour..."

But it is fading again, his voice drifting off into the distance as if he is walking away as he speaks. Come back Bugsy don't leave me like this, only it isn't him who is leaving....

It should have been scrubbed from scratch. When the choppers had gone and left you in the clearing and the company began its trek in the pouring rain, it could have been said that there was ample time. On the drawing boards back at Nui Dat where the Task Force masters laid out their tactics, everything said it could have been done. Fly in, five thousand metres, cordon and sweep enemy encampment, mop up and fly back to Nui Dat. A good solid day's work. Perfectly feasible in theory. But even as you began the march, the world closed in on you. In the shadows of the stormclouds, in the pounding cascades of rain, in the dense shrouded jungle, you walking into a dim narrowing world.

"Any chance of an appeal against the light?" Nigel asked grimly.

It was clear after the first hour that you weren't going to get there in time.

Visions of men trudging in the deluge, teeth bared, eyes squinted, constantly troubled by their footing on the uneven sloppy ground. Your clothes and gear were saturated, utterly waterlogged, doubling

47

the weight. Even under the roof of the jungle, the curtain of rain was so heavy that visibility was often restricted to a few yards, and you wondered how anyone could possibly know where they were going. You had walked through heavy rainstorms before, the sudden torrents that hit daily, at a predictable time, flooding everything in a matter of minutes, then just as suddenly stop, the sun would reappear, steam would rise and in no time it would be as hot and dry as if the rain had never happened. This was different. The rain went on and on, thunder erupted almost continually and lightning streaked the sky—a flickering florescence in the murk. The jungle was all instantaneous shadows and indefinable shapes that kept the nerves on edge. The thunder rang in your ears and set your hearts beating at an erratic pace.

"The Great War Gods are angry," The Greyman said forbiddingly.

In the third hour, they ran into trouble—a swamp with trees so dense that you had to cut your way through. The maps were unclear—there was no way of telling what might be gained by attempting to go around this watery forest and the fear of navigational errors that might be induced by such a detour left no alternative but to chop a path straight through. There was the advantage that these soft watertrees could be sliced through with a single blow of a machete and most blows lopped several at a time. In a wild frenzy, the lead section hacked away at the wall while the rest of you stood waiting in the green and yellow tunnel they created, up to your calves in slime and boughs and giant leaves, fighting a ceaseless war with the leeches.

The leeches were mostly a minor irritation except that they had a nasty habit of entering the channel of the prick and rendering the owner a screaming wreck until he was got to hospital and a tiny umbrella device was employed to extract the invader. You shuddered at the thought of that dreadful contrivance, and the waiting men needed no encouragement to light a cigarette every ten minutes, lower their daks and burn off the dozen or so new infiltrators on their legs. The cigarettes were regulation issue with the US ration packs, and, like the Vietnamese children, the company's handful of resolute non-smokers also had a preference for Salems. But most gasped Chesterfields and Camels.

There was too a dread of being bitten on the bum by the watersnakes...

You took your place at the head of the line. Under Hatrack's impatient urging, Nigel, Bugsy and Sniffer chopped frantically until exhausted, you, Greyman and Alby Dunshea took over, and then the mighty Snowy had a furious session all on his own since his huge backswing allowed no space for anyone else. You got to hold Mabel for those few minutes—a rare concession. Snowy swung and slashed way beyond the strength of the other men and then, as if in divine acknowledgment of his effort, daylight suddenly appeared through the broad leaves. Snowy sheathed his machete and hurled his whole body at the wall and ploughed right on through, disappearing out there somewhere with a massive splash. They broke through behind him, Hatrack clawing his way past you, and his momentary jubilance was quickly swamped by gloom.

"Ohhh no," they moaned.

There, spreading away before you in all directions was a vast shallow lake, dotted with clumps of weeds and watertrees, stretching ahead of you to the horizon.

"We'll have to go through it," Hatrack gritted, mostly to himself in his despair at the soggy mess the expedition was becoming.

"We can't," Nigel protested. "We don't know how deep it is."

Hatrack flared with fierce impatience. "That's tough. We'll just have to find the shallow parts. We're way behind time already. Nigel, get your blokes together and lead us off."

"Which way?" Nigel asked, staring in frustration at the drowned world ahead.

Hatrack eyed him bleakly and cast a firm directing hand. "Straight across."

Hatrack ploughed back through the tunnel to consult his SAS guides and officers, while Nigel, grimacing angrily, turned toward you.

"Awright, saddle up, you guys. It's bath time!"

In single file, you weaved your way through that lake of foul mud

49

like a huge snake, up to your knees and sometimes your waists in the odorous slime, struggling forward at the point of exhaustion, pushed on by the knowledge that when you stopped you immediately began to sink even deeper. There were the roots of the mangroves and reeds down there just below the bed of mud and that was all spared you from sinking to God knows what abysmal depths. Sniffer led the way until it was discovered that, lightly built, he was able to traverse ground over which heavier men could not follow.

"We need a bigger bloke up front," Nigel said and looked at you.

"What about Snowy. He's twice my size."

"Need him here. Away you go, Yogi."

It was tricky stuff in the lead. You stayed as close to each outcrop as you could, edging around it and then crossing to the next. Every step had to be tested first, probing with the boot for something to put your foot on, giving it a bit of weight, if it held, begin the next step. Directly behind, Nigel puzzled over your true course—at every turn you looked back and he checked the compass and offered the direction you should go, but you were rarely able to go that way. His attempts to make corrections for the constant deviations could only be guesswork.

After Nigel, Snowy struggled along with Mabel, following your footsteps exactly. Mabel was giving him hell—normally he carried her the way most men carried a rifle, but now her bulk was a major problem and he teetered along at the brink of collapse, worn down by his effort with the machete, frustrated by the number of times Mabel's bipod tangled in the mangrove vines, irritated by roots which had tripped him up, exasperated when the uneven footing bogged him down. Sniffer and Bugsy spent half their time gripping Snowy by the armpits to try and keep him afloat.

"He's a genius, that fuckin' Hatrack," Snowy thundered angrily. "No wonder we fuckin' love him so!"

Nigel looked back toward him, his own humour completely worn: "What the fuck are you bitchin' about now?"

"Wadda yer fuckin' reckon!" Snowy savaged back. "First he has us clearin' a fuckin' highway through that crap, now he navigates us

50

into this fuckin' slop! He needs his fuckin' balls cut out, if he's got any!"

Nigel eyed his gunner with despair—it signalled the end of all reason.

"Bugsy. Give Snowy a break with the gun for a while."

Bugsy, a receiver of life's cruellest blows, only nodded and stepped forward and Snowy, so obsessively jealous of Mabel, this time gave her up gladly.

"Hungry for fuckin' kills, that's what he is," Snowy continued to rage. "Couldn't give a shit what happens to us poor fuckers as long as we get him some fuckin' kills and thrill the bigwigs back at Task Force."

Soon, Bugsy was equally wretched.

At the front of the line, you suddenly found that all strength was gone from your legs and you began sinking, slowly at first, then rapidly as you floundered about, and finally sucked right up to your chest. You could find no air to cry for help, and kept on silently going down until Nigel, turning from the Bugsy-Snowy distraction, saw your plight and plunged forward. You felt him grab you by the collar: you could only flail in no reasonable attempt to save yourself whatsoever, and Nigel, unable to pull against the suction, could do no more than hang on desperately until Greyman and Alby Dunshea surged forward and helped him drag you out. They propped you up against the trunk of a mangrove and left you gasping and helpless.

"Why didn't you say something, you dill?" Nigel muttered.

Still, there was no air available for speech.

"He was tryin' to drown himself," Snowy snarled. "Only fuckin' way out of this fuckin' mess."

"You bastards spoil all your fun," you gasped feebly.

"Awright, Alby. Take the lead."

"You know I always lead us into trouble..." Dunshea warned.

"We are already in trouble, dickhead," Nigel growled.

They moved on, Alby Dunshea taking the lead with a glance that knew that soon your condition would be his, and you leaned for a while as they went by. Soon after, Kinross's section came through and took the lead and you slipped back down the line but it wasn't any easier there.

...now forever later and your can still smell that slimy lake. For hour upon hour you have been soaked by continuous rain yet still the stink of the mud prevails, as if it has permeated your whole body. You seemed to wander in that vile morass forever, now forever ago. Now lying in the rain and the darkness and still the storm raging on. But you can hear voices and sounds, the ring of machetes clear and sharp as men cut away at the trees. Sure, making a chopper pad, or at least clearing the canopy enough to allow one access overhead. Fuckin' useless. Couldn't fly in this shit anyway.

Other men moving, talking, but it is as if it is all going on around you and you were not there to be seen or noticed; a fish peering out of its aquarium, unable to penetrate the glass by word or deed.

"You there, Bugsy?" that voice that is yours but somehow not part of you calls croakily.

"Course I'm still fuckin' here."

"What time is it?"

"What do you want to know the fuckin' time for?"

"I dunno. I just..." but no, that isn't what you meant to ask, something different, not the time, but it's faded now, like everything else.

Then Bugsy says, perhaps as an afterthought: "You were out again for a while there, maybe fifteen minutes."

"Yeah. It keeps coming and going. But it was today, wasn't it, that we were in the swamp."

Bugsy chuckled: "Yeah, Yogi. About seven or eight hours ago. Seems a bloody lot longer, doesn't it."

"Pity we ever got out of it."

"Well, that's one way of looking at it, I suppose."

Finally you stumbled up onto firm ground, men dragging them-selves free of the slime and collapsing without even the strength to help their struggling mates up the bank. All, that was, except Hatrack, athletic and maniacal, who came bounding out of the swamp like The Creature from the Black Lagoon and was amongst them in a fanatical frenzy. "Come on, come on, you men! Get off your bums! We're running out of time! On your feet! Come on, let's go! Let's go!"

You barrelled through the scrub for now the ground was flat and the scrub light and the going suddenly unbelievably easy after what you had been through. There was a long gentle upward incline that went on for miles, the footing was firm in spite of the rain, and the lead sections could open up and rush along, a long striding desperate pace that had you tail-waggers struggling to keep up. All that you knew of tactics and security was abandoned now—caution, quietness, alertness, these things so inherent to your lives, were forsaken in the blind rush to reach the objective while there was still daylight. You heard that Hatrack himself was now in the lead, along with other more reckless section leaders, for certainly he would never have persuaded someone like Nigel to travel at this pace, charging through the forest, desperate amid so many desperations to make up time as you ran with the day toward its end. And the storm too, seemingly apace with you, strove toward a new intensity—the rain streaking through this more open canopy, the lightning ripping open the dense grey sky, the thunder erupting about you like shell bursts. It was, Nigel said, like a cavalry charge without the benefit of horses; and they came swooping down like riders on the storm to unleash a manmade ravage of their own that rivalled the violence and anger of the typhoon and tore men's lives as the wind lashed the trees...

...still feeling the strain of that forced march too, in the weary leg muscles in spite of all that has happened since. And the pain that isn't really pain in the numbness that secretes it. It's the drugs, of course, setting your mind wandering, drifting in a maze of visions real and imagined but the worst ones are real. But for it all, you can still feel the exhaustion that wracks your entire body—neither pain nor numbness nor drugs could completely overwhelm the stress of a body where every muscle, every bone, every joint, seemed to ache, strained beyond all of its limits.

"You still there, Bugsy?"

No answer!

Panic immediately sweeps through you. That dread feeling that you have been left alone, deserted, may be dead... It is so cold, so void, although there is the rain that is somehow a comfort, contact with life. So helpless, to be left like this. But hang on, there are sounds, men calling, moving, chopping, but they are all so far away, so remote.

"Hey Bugsy, where are you?"

"I'm here, fuck you Yogi. It's alright."

Not exactly here. He is a little way off still.

"I thought you were gone..."

"I was just having a piss, do you mind?"

You hear the rustle as he returns to his place, kneeling beside you, you can almost make out his darker form.

"What's going on?"

"It's alright, Yogi. Don't worry, mate."

"I was out of it again, huh?"

"Just for a few minutes."

Then there are other figures, looming over the top, and Bugsy stands to talk to them. You listen to the distance voices that are right there, as if you are at the bottom of a well.

"Private Griffin, is it?"

That is Bulldog Doyle.

"Yeah," says Bugsy. He doesn't sound too happy. Not at all encouraging in the circumstances.

"Leg," Ten Days's voice says. "No break but he's lost gallons of blood and still losing more. He'll have to be one of the first to go. Is he still conscious, Bugsy?"

"Keeps wandering in and out."

Sounds so strange, listening to people talk about you as if you didn't exist anymore.

"Very well, Corporal Hollis. Do what you can for him," says a different voice. You know that one too. It belongs to that bastard Hatrack...

"Piss off, Hatrack!"

That voice belonged to Yogi Griffin.

There is a shocked silence. Then Hatrack says. "Now, Private Griffin. Just because you're wounded doesn't mean..."

"Get lost you great ugly pile of shit or I'll get up and kick you to death you rotten shithead bloodhungry bastard!"

The second stunned pause is longer.

"I don't think you'll be kicking anybody for some considerable time, Private Griffin," Bulldog Doyle says coldly, but then, further away. "We'd better be moving on, Major."

"I want you to take disciplinary action, CSM..."

"Just move on, Major, before this gets out of hand."

And they are drifting away, or is it you. Test it out. "Bastard! You bloodthirsty killhappy bastard!"

Them drifting away this time.

It is amazing just how much better you suddenly feel, and Bugsy is chuckling as he gets down beside you. "Nicely handled, Yogi. Discreet. Charming. Tactful."

"I thought so."

"I bet you got yourself wounded just especially to be able to get away with that."

"It was almost worth it, Bugsy. Almost worth it."

It was all Hatrack's fault. It was his fault for going on with the mission when conditions went so heavily against its chances of success. He could have called it off at any time, and should have, but his desperation to succeed would not allow that. And when they arrived, there was too little light left—although much lost time had been made up in that final frantic rush, the storm had brought darkness prematurely and there was simply not enough light. But Hatrack was determined to go on with it, and he did. Ten Platoon was despatched in a wide arc to lay ambushes on the far side of the camp. The rest of the company would sweep through and Charlie, should they be there, would bug out as was their custom and be caught in those Ten Platoon ambushes. Good enough in theory. But there was no time to recce and try and determine what they might have been up against. It was all done with maximum haste on the principle that the sooner you got in there, the more light you would have to see what you were doing. In those last seconds before darkness was complete, you went into the camp, tired, frustrated men, reflexes dulled, minds slow to respond to their senses.

Peering through the gloom, you trudged unevenly, and could never have explained how you knew your senses were trying to tell you something. Mute senses, unable to get their messages through, could only raise your awareness until you knew you were looking for something in particular, something odd, something that did not fit, without knowing what it might have been nor even what caused you to look. Every nerve-end seemed exposed, nakedly outside your body like antennae. Your eyes bulged as they strove to fit visual form to sensation, and then you could see it too, something alien amid the tangle of branches and leaves. You moved on, holding your place in the line, concentrating, confounded by the failing light.

There was a straight vertical edge of blackness in there—man-made. With every step it became clearer—a thatched hut, so perfectly assimilated into its surroundings that you were ten yards from it before you knew it was there. Ears strained now, but nothing could be heard over the rain and the rustling tread of the men either side of you. You wished they could be quieter now. You looked left and there was Sniffer, touching his nose with his finger. And that was it, that distinct pungent odour that prevailed whenever they were around. The hut, the smell, the sixth sense too—yes, you had it in the neck alright—all of which told you what you and everyone else should have know minutes before. They were there. The bastards were in there!

But the long tedious journey had taken its toll, numbing senses, slowing reflexes, disallowing the sluggish brain to respond. You won-

56

dered how many other men knew Charlie was in there waiting in those last crucial seconds when something, anything, done or spoken, might have made others more prepared, might have saved lives. There might have been many who knew, like you did, but couldn't get their exhausted bodies to react. So they just went on in and the trap closed about you, and your dulled reactions allowed it to happen uncaringly.

The sharp, sudden flash and with it the twin detonations, and your brain screamed: rocket! The most terrible of your fears yet three or four more were launched and hit in that instant between recognition and reaction. You hit the deck fast—and there were more white flashes and bursts of yellow light, each sandwiched between the blasts, launching and striking. More of them, bloody tons of the bastards, but hang on. The danger is wide, well wide. Perhaps a safe distance. Relatively... The attack is on Twelve Platoon, fifty yards away to the left, and even as you realise it, the first splatterings of gunshots can be heard in response, rising swiftly to a crescendo.

You start to get up, looking toward Nigel even though you already know what his instruction will be. "Keep moving," Nigel breathes softly, more an expelling of air than real words, but every man immediately responds. You stand, returning your attention to the huts. They could be in there too, waiting with the fuckin' rockets.

Now all of Eleven Platoon was on the move again, fanned out — no groups for easy targets. All eyes and ears are intent on the shadows and silence directly ahead, shutting out the unseen horror away to the flank. Those bloody rockets—just to hear them was terrifying enough but now, had you listened, you could have heard the cries of men too, their screams of pain, their warnings to each other, orders shouted and reshouted as the clamour of gunfire drowned them out. Pitted against the barrage of rockets, the desperate gunshots of Twelve Platoon sounded pitifully inadequate. And you and the rest of Eleven Platoon are so near and yet so uninvolved, your body heavy with helplessness. All you can do is push on quietly into the camp.

And then you have gone too far, and the camp is all around you. In front is an area cleared to ground level. A dozen small stilted huts stand threateningly in the open. No cover in there, and no going around it either, but it would be suicide to go further if they were waiting. You stop, uninstructed, as everyone stops, eyes and ears straining for some sign, some warning, of movement, of danger. But there is only the dreadful tumult away to the left. Shut it out. Think about this. Eleven Platoon is too far forward, you are sure, and the gap between you and the stricken Twelve Platoon too wide. Hatrack and the support group, coming up behind Twelve Platoon to back them up, are probably equally pinned down, and that leaves you and this open ground and these huts. The next move is with Holly and the little man is in a quandary. The instinct is to rush down to Twelve Platoon's aid, but you must clear this area first, or you'll have rockets up your bums. If you get pinned down too the whole company is fucked. Holly dithers, looking at his section leaders who glare back silently. Finally, it is left to Nigel. "Awright, fuck you Holly. Do you want me to fucking go in there or don't you?"

There really wasn't an alternative. Twelve Platoon and Company were crippled, outgunned and pinned down at the edge of the camp while you were unopposed in the middle. Charlie was staying and fighting back, perhaps a rearguard group with a good supply of rockets providing the superiority they always waited for. In any case, it was in your hands to solve the problem. Hit this area hard and fast and clear it, then strike right down through the middle of the camp and assail its defenders from the flank. A reckless plan but if it all went wrong, bad luck. All the men around the lieutenant glared, putting the pressure on, and he had no choice. "Okay, let's go," he said belatedly. "Straight up the guts."

There is no need for anyone to relay the order—they were away like sprinters, bursting into the open, going straight at those huts. Four section automatically split into three, Alby Dunshea and you to the left, Nigel and Greyman right, Snowy, Sniffer and Bugsy staying where they were, giving cover. It is that blind run again, to make ground for there is no cover except the huts and you go straight at them. If you hit trouble, you sort it out there and then, but in any case, there isn't. One man moves, the other covers, until finally you're under the huts and still no shooting.

"Nobody home," Nigel bellows to Holly, and immediately wheels around while his section falls into line abreast and the other two sections either side, facing toward the savage battle over there in the dark jungle, striding down through the camp at a furious pace.

It is harrowing to go through the camp like this, past so many huts and bunkers that should be explored, cleared, blasted with grenades, but there is no time. With you goes the knowledge that sooner or later you must be fired upon—the camp is huge, you can see, several hundred population, but most are gone. There's just this stubborn rearguard force, concentrated in one part of the camp and you go swiftly, foolishly bold, defying all tensions. It is an aggressor's game now, and all you can do is hope that when the firing starts it will be someone else in their sights.

And when it does happen—when suddenly the white light blossoms ahead and sends the rocket screaming over to strike somewhere behind, it is mostly relief you feel. You plunge to the ground, far too late, showered by flying bits of bark and dirt as another rocket hits closer. Someone begins swearing loudly as you do yourself, but this is better—the nervewracking anxiety of the unknown is past and action will come striding into its place.

You begin firing, adding to the torrent of tracers streaking into the base of the hut from where the rockets were given their brief deadly life. You see Snowy flat on his belly, quivering all over as he lays down a deluge of fire from Mabel, and further wide, Alby Dunshea, changing magazines with swift, shaking hands. There are no other men within your range of vision, but the flashes and brilliant yellow slits of tracers tell you they were there. You empty your mag and grapple another out of your pouch, clip it on and slip the empty away. But don't fire again for a moment—don't waste the ammo. Who knows how long this will go on? After that initial outburst, the shooting eases off. There were four or five rockets, all fired immediately—they probably don't have any more. Some incoming gunfire, but maybe even that is really coming from Twelve Platoon. You hug the ground, waiting and watching for more specific targets. There are none. Calmer now, and you notice, or re-notice, that the rain is pouring down again and you are wet and uncomfortable. Steam sizzles from the barrel of your rifle. You take a breath and wait two or three seconds—a year at a time like this.

Something dances by—a bright spirited tracer bouncing off the ground and spinning away, glowing pink. It catches your eye only momentarily but you ignore it, even though you know it could have torn the life out of your body. There is a glimpsed shadow down by that hut—perhaps a shadow, perhaps a man, you pump a few rounds off at it. Three, four, keep count now, don't get caught short, the thump of the butt against your shoulder a reminder of numbers. Over there, a muzzle flash—three four five rounds at that, nine down, half mag. The incoming is depleting—they are losing their taste for the fight and bugging out like they were supposed to do in the first place.

Someone is screaming! Right beside you and you look that way. Alby Dunshea! He's rolled onto his back, muddy hands slapped to his face, white teeth bared. That long, awful scream and then he stops for breath and screams again. No, no, not Alby Dunshea, not poor slow-wit Dunshea. Crabwise, you slither over to his side and pounce upon his body as he begins to convulse, threshing maniacally on the muddy ground. Blood bursts through his fingers still clutched to his face.

"Medic!" you bellow at the top of your voice, without any real hope of being heard amid this racket. Grab him by the wrists and get the hands away from his face, get a look at it. A great hole there, right on the cheekbone. Shit! No time for sympathies though. He's screaming again, mouth stretched wide eyes open staring, body in fierce spasms. Screaming, screaming but your ears are numbing to it. Screaming means still alive. Your fumbling hands and useless fingers tear at his breastpocket and drag out the shelldressing, rip the wrapper away with your teeth. Your hands covered in blood, washed away by the rain, bloodied again as you press the padding to his face, and he twists and tries to get away as if you were smothering him with a pillow.

"Easy Alby easy," you gasp and grab his neck roughly, winding the trailing gauze around his head again and again.

"Medic!"

Figures racing past you, got to get on, don't waste time on wounded and dead, Snowy lumbers by, Sniffer behind like a faithful hound.

"They're bugging out, we got 'em running," voices are yelling.

"After them! Keep moving!" Nigel's voice roars.

Dunshea is down, and that scream you no longer hear ripping through to your spine and then suddenly he is silent and still. You kneel there, paralysed yourself, staring in horror. Scream again, Alby, scream again. Someone comes sliding like a baseball player, and hands attack your hastily applied dressing.

"I've got him," Ten Days says.

"Is he dead?" you gasp.

"I've got him. Piss off Yogi."

But you can't move, can't go, not like this, you have to know.

"Is he dead, fuck you?"

While Ten Days frantically hunts for pulses.

"No. He's alive. Now fuck off and let me do my job."

You drag yourself to your feet, backing away. Take it easy, Yogi Bear. You're panicking. Cool it. A long last glance. You can see Alby Dunshea's chest moving while Ten Days works at the dressing. Poor Dunshea. Then turning, and onward in pursuit of the battle...

...poor Alby Dunshea. Too slow; too awkward to get out of his own way. And that screaming lodged in your brain, as if it was your own.

"Hey Bugsy, you still there?"

"Yes, bugger you, Yogi. I'm still here."

"Thought you went away again."

"I'm still here. What do you keep waking up for? There's nothing to see."

"How's Alby?"

"He's alright..."

"You sure. Looked bad."

"He's alright. Better than you are."

"In the face. He got it in the face."

"Bloody lucky, actually. They think it was a bullet that bounced right off his cheekbone. Just a glancing blow..."

"I thought he was dead."

"No. Just a little bit uglier, if that's possible."

And then someone, Dorset, CHQ signaller, calling. "Choppers are in the area now!"

"Fire the flares!" Bulldog Doyle roars and instantly there is light and movement and giant shadows everywhere. That black world is suddenly as bright as daylight, huge monstrous shadows looming as the brilliant phosphorescence of the flares pierce through the jungle and the storm.

"They see us!" Dorset yells. "Dust-off locked in!"

But the brilliance of the light is too much for failed eyes like mine, you turn your head away and closed it out.

"Won't be long now, Yogi," Bugsy says.

But there is no longer any such thing as time.

Running toward the battle from the rear, you are confronted with a scene that seems unrelated to the death and destruction it is supposed to convey. With the night fully descended and the rain almost horizontal before the force of the wind, the white flickers of muzzle flashes, the elongated sparks of tracers, the blossoms of explosions, all seem from your detached position more like a carnival fireworks display. Your ears are now oblivious to the detonations and the fever of action is in full command of your senses—you are no longer inclined to duck and flinch, instead running forward boldly, the yells of the men, screams of pain, of warning, of instruction, all seem to have lost their impact and urgency. It might just as well be the joyful shrieks and laughter of a distant funpark. Over it comes the thunder and lightning, indistinguishable from the explosions of artillery summoned in support, all so continuous that it blends into a meaningless babbling eruption. Toward this madman's monstrous orchestration, you run on, your eyes and ears listening for one thing only, the voice and movement of Nigel, to guide you to where you ought to have been...

Flying through the air, suddenly, inexplicably, upended in midair and hitting the ground in a flurry of arms and legs.

"Jesus Fucking Christ Almighty!"

There seemed to be a heavy crunch behind you, or did you trip, or what. Doesn't matter. You bounce up virtually ending on your feet and still running. No time to think about it—if hurt you wouldn't be running, you're running therefore not hurt. Your skinned knees and elbows remain with you as a reminder of the spill though it will be some time before you realise that you have just been floored by an explosion that must have been pretty fucking close.

"Snowy have a fuckin' look to your right!"

Nigel! His voice hoarse and quaking, but it's him alright. The long slits of tracers so numerous they must be Mabel, streaking across your path ahead. You drop to one knee and see the momentary image of fleeing figures at the end of Mabel's fiery tongue, and pump off a few shots that way yourself. Seventeen. Give 'em the last two. Change mags. Your breath is completely gone from the hectic run but you can see Nigel now, over there appearing fleetingly like an apparition in the flashes, directing traffic.

"Keep moving, keep moving, keep moving," he is yelling. Back to the fold.

Something streaked by and splattered mud in your face, but you can't see anything to fire back at. The incoming is almost non-existent now.

"We gotta get closer," Nigel shouts excitedly. He too can see the opposition is lessening.

"Awright, Snowy, give us cover. The rest of you, let's go!"

And you're away, stumbling the first few strides as your boots strive for traction on the slippery ground. Running, hunched forward, over to that post, stop, look, shadows, fire at them, keep count, across to that hut, go, go, go! Other men running, firing, dashing here and there, until there's only you and the firing tails off.

"We got 'em running! Look at 'em go. Give 'em something to go on with!"

Then you can hear other voices, different voices from further wide. Holly, calling urgently. "Don't go any further, Nigel. We're right on top of Twelve Platoon. Prop and hold ground."

You go to ground and lay there, watching, waiting, changing mags again. And a lull—inexplicable really—suddenly hangs over you as if Holly had commanded it. Waiting, waiting, something must happen and does. Firing way to the flank, off in the direction, you realise, of the Ten Platoon ambushes, transferring the battle to a new location.

You lay in the rain and sudden cold, shivering uncontrollably. The weather seems to be turning worse or maybe you are becoming more aware of it. Greyman's Great War Gods, as if angered by the brief but violent conflict, have whipped up this fierce barrage of their own, the wind leans on the trees and roars through the jungle like an enraged animal; and the driving rain and the thunder and lightning rendered sight, sound and a cruel chill factor as evidence of their wrath. You lay on the ground and remembered then the things you had seen and done, and for the first time that day, you were really frightened.

From miles away at Nui Dat and The Horseshoe, they blasted shells into the air that streaked overhead and pounded the jungle all around in a one mile radius, adding further, you imagined, to the troubles of the fleeing Viet Cong. Down in the camp, the victors lay with frayed nerves, jumping at each explosion and then cursing their own edginess.

You got a fag alight and it was better then, and then the voices again, even more comfort: there was Nigel, calling toward his men as the other section leaders were doing, but strangely the only voice you heard was his.

"Awright, anyone hurt?"

And you remembered and answered. "Alby Dunshea was hit. The medics picked him up."

"Alive?"

"Yeah. Nasty one but."

"Snowy. Sniffer."

"We're over here. We're okay."

"Billy. Bugsy?"

"No worries, Nigel."

"Awright. Check ammo."

You settled down. Greyman and Bugsy were right behind you, just a few feet away and you turned toward them. "Did we win?" Greyman asked.

But there was a puzzled look on Bugsy's face, glimpsed in the flashes of light.

"Hey Yogi. What's wrong with your leg?"

Now that he mentioned it, there did seem to be something strange about it. You rolled over, reaching down to grope about. There was a clamminess in your boot like someone had filled it with mud and it felt as if someone was holding you firmly by the calf muscle. When you tried to do the same, your hand went right in amid a mess of warm spongy stuff.

"Hey, hey!" you were yelling. "I'm fuckin' bleeding."

Bugsy came scurrying over, squatted there and seized your trouser leg, ripping it open. He looked at you and you looked at him.

"Hey Nigel, Yogi's been shot."

"What by?"

"A fuckin' bullet."

"I mean what happened, dickhead."

"I'm buggered if I know," was the best you could manage. You were beginning to feel strange, nauseous. It was probably the shock, more than anything. Nigel sprang across and had his pencil torch alight.

"Fuck me dead. You dumb bastard. Why didn't you say something?"

You wanted to explain your unlikely story that you didn't know anything about it, but your lower jaw did not want to assist with speaking. All of a sudden, nothing seemed to be working properly.

"Greyman," Nigel was saying from a million miles away. "Go find a medic. This is fuckin' serious."

Serious it might have been but you didn't know and didn't care. Just let it all fade away, and fade away it did...

...rising up again, floating on an invisible ocean, lurching out of one nightmare into another. This is a frenzied world of shifting dazzling lights, of unbelievable noise and shattering furious violence as a huge monster with one brilliant eye seems to be hanging magically, terribly, overhead, dancing awkwardly against the backdrop of a rainswept sky, intermittently illuminated by the lightning. The one fiery eye of this dreadful flying dragon, more brilliant and more directed than the lightning, seems to be searching the earth for its prey, and you are that prey.

All about you can see silhouettes of men moving in the light of that great eye, men moving in desperate, frantic haste, their hair and clothes lashed by the forces of two different winds—the horizontal gale of the storm and the vertical downdraft of the monster.

You move your head to try and gain some comprehension, some sensual foothold amid this berserk scene of trees and men thrashing in the grip of some massive attacker. You want again the peace of waking up and finding Bugsy there. Instead there is only this hellish madness and sharp stinging pains from your leg to let you know that this is real, that this is really happening.

"Alright Bugsy, let's have yours."

Two figures, one Bugsy, the other possibly Sniffer, lean over you head and foot and somehow raise you up—only then does it occur to you that you have been lying on some sort of makeshift stretcher.

"Jeez, he's a heavy bastard," you hear Sniffer groan.

"Coulda been worse," you hear yourself answer. "It coulda been Snowy."

"Oh no, he's awake again," Bugsy groans.

"You sure you don't wanna sleep though this, Yogi?" Sniffer asks. Sleep through what?

They move you across to a point directly below the wobbling chopper with its single dazzling landing light, hanging in the sky just above treetop height. The wind chills right through your clothing, and there is a great sloshing puddle of water with you in the indentation of the stretcher—all of a sudden you cannot shake the idea that you are drowning. In a sea of blood...

If only you could be warm, it is so cold. They lower you to the ground, fully exposed to the sleet blasted downward by the chopper blades, and other men rush in, brushing Sniffer and Bugsy aside. Without consideration for your condition, these panicky fellows heave you from the rudimentary stretcher to another with a steel frame.

"Hey, take it easy. I'm a casualty," you cry but no one heeds you.

Straps fastened about your body, hooks being clipped to cables, everything double tightened, and all done to a chorus of fumbles and curses while rainwater drips from the chin of someone you don't know, splattering disgustingly in your unshielded face. The speed and unexpectedness of it outpaces your brain—before you can protest, it's all done and you're jerked rudely off the ground. You look around desperately for a friend.

"Hey Bugsy, you there?"

"Don't go pissing the bed, Yogi."

And you're swinging wildly away and he was gone.

Now you are in full possession of the giant hovering cyclops, swinging about in midair and being unsteadily drawn toward that overpowering eye at the centre of a world that is beginning to revolve faster and faster. The rain slices across your face and the downdraft squints your eyes and you spin around and around with the clawlike branches of the trees lashing out at you hungrily. The cable bows and tightens with each jerk, surely it will not stand this strain and snap and send you plummeting to the ground. Trussed up like a roast pig, tied down and helpless while every wrench of the cable pulls you closer to the chopper which means further from the ground, where death yawns should that cable snap.

Heaving upward and upward until there is nothing but the rotating black underbelly of the chopper that by now seems to be spinning as fast as its own rotors. Everything is quivering and shaking. You close your eyes and are instantly gripped by nausea—the horror is worse unseen. What a bloody ridiculous thing to let them do to you!

Then you are right under the chopper—you could reach out and grab one of the landing struts and assure your safety if you had a free arm. Two more jerks of the cable and your stretcher clatters over the strut, and a helmeted head bobs out of the cabin, an arm stretched to steady the cable. You are drawn alongside and the crewman hauls the stretcher in, sliding it across the floor and snapping its feet into the locking grooves on the floor that you always noticed but never realised what they were for.

Once there you find the constant jolting of the chopper no better than that of the cable; the machine unbalanced by the high winds and the need for constant hovering. Choppers aren't supposed to be able to fly in these conditions. Maybe they can't...You are sure that if the floor tilts far enough, you will slide out, stretcher and all, into the empty air and there will be nothing you can do to save yourself, all trussed up like this.

But then they are away, the rotor blades developing that frenetic flapping sound and the whole machine bumping wildly as it strives for altitude against the buffeting wind. Beside you, another stretcher locked in the floor grooves, and several men seated, wearing bandages impossibly huge. No one you can recognise under these circumstances.

Otherwise there is only the twin domes of the pilot's helmets as they struggle to keep flying, and outside the murky, saturated sky when lightning illuminates it, and otherwise black nothing. Your leg begins to pain—the drugs are wearing off. It would be nice to be unconscious again, but even that doesn't seem to be working. All you can do is lie there, and try to think of how good it would be when the fear and discomfort ended and you would be safely tucked into bed in Vung Tau hospital.

6. Streetscene in Saigon

You felt utterly ridiculous but so, you supposed, would anyone else who possessed a shred of dignity. The place was a busy street in the bustling heart of the Cholon district of Saigon where stood the Australian billet, a former hotel converted for the purpose of housing those diggers lucky enough to be posted to that city. Immediately to the left of the wide portals of that edifice was a sentry box, looking rather like a country dunny with the walls missing, except that it had been sandbagged up to chest height. Inside the sentry box stood Yogi the Bear, looking straight and stern, complete with rifle and radio and wearing not only a steel helmet but also—heaven forbid—a flak jacket. All in all, it was a fine spectacle of Downunder ferocity.

And piteously, that was exactly why you were there. Large signs in Vietnamese at either end of the building warned passing pedestrians and motorists that under no circumstances were they allowed to pause or halt outside this building, and that anyone who behaved in a suspicious manner would be shot. You were to ensure that these rulings were properly observed by the indigenous population and, if it came to it, do the shooting. Great fun. Although, in reality, your orders did not match the certainty of the signs. If anyone stopped on the street within your range of vision, you were to call upon them to move on at once, and had even taught you the Vietnamese expression—*Di Di Mau!* and if not obeyed immediately, level weapon and shout menacingly *Mau lên không tôi bán!* which they assured you meant *Quick or I'll shoot!* If they still did not comply immediately, you were to fire a shot in the air, high above the line of the buildings across the street. This would effectively break out the other five members of the guard, presently lounging about inside the building, who would deploy to

69

meet any threat. You were not allowed to shoot anyone unless you positively considered there to be a life-threatening danger.

So far you had got to fire just once, but it was worth it. A car, one of the innumerable yellow and blue Renault taxis that plagued the street along with a sea of bicycles, motor-scooters, rickshaws and pedestrians, had halted directly across the way. A man got out and you bellowed at him. The man looked at you in faint surprise. You roared your second instruction to which this cheeky little Vietnamese offered the Frenchman's shrug. Blam! The shot echoed around the rooftops deafeningly and in one instant, the street was completely clear. By the time the members of the guard burst into the street, you were crippled with laughter. They were just in time to see a man push his Renault around the far corner, giving substantiation to your action. Otherwise, the street was devoid of life.

The logic behind all this nonsense was the not unreasonable thinking that city-based troops were not capable to defending themselves and hence, every week, a bunch of infantrymen were collected from reinforcement groups or the convalescent centre or even Nui Dat, and rostered on this duty. After four weeks in the hospital at Vung Tau, you were glad of the break. The duty roster was twenty-four hours on, twenty-four off. Those twenty-four hours freely roaming the city made it all worthwhile. And in addition, it offered acceptable light duties to test out your leg. You hardly even limped any more.

So you stood at your guardpost like a chocolate soldier and mused on the fact that in less than an hour, your duty would be finished for the next day.

"Go on, you silly old bag. Keep moving."

What you needed least of all was someone you knew to catch you in the midst of all this absurdity.

"Do you reckon the sign says *Beware of the Dog!?*" Bugsy Norris asked.

"*Beware of the Bear,*" Sniffer Gibson corrected.

Oh gawd!

They came with their huge grins to lean on the sandbags to either side of the sentry box.

"Go on, piss off you two," you protested. "Can't you read the sign?"

"Vietnamese is all Greek to me," Sniffer laughed.

"It says if you don't move on, I get to shoot you."

"Must be worth gettin' shot if you end up doing important jobs like this," Bugsy chuckled.

"And what, may I ask, are you two yahoos doing here?"

"You hear that, Sniffer. We risk our necks coming halfway across the war zone to visit him and he calls us yahoos."

"Bloody terrible business, Bugsy. Certainly won't be winning many hearts and minds with nasty types like him around."

An hour later you were sitting in the bar, all three now in civilian dress, and explanations were being offered.

"So there we were," Sniffer was saying. "with three day's leave in Vungers and getting bored already. Thought we'd go visit our old mate Yogi Bear in hospital. We arrive, but lo! he's not there. We find out he's living it up in the wilds of Saigon. So we dumped the flowers and ate the chocolates ourselves and headed for the nearest bar."

"Where," Bugsy picked up the tale "we happened upon a chap who was a Yank pilot and feeling lonely and he said all we had to do was go to the airport and walk out on the tarmac and ask around until we found a plane going to Saigon and go and ask the pilot for a ride. Which we did, and here we are."

"Mad bastards," you shook your head in disapproval when in fact you were very pleased. "To tell you the truth, the only difference between Vung Tau and Saigon is that Saigon is bigger. And it doesn't have a beach."

"If it's bigger, then it has more bars and more women to choose from," Bugsy declared. "Which makes me wonder why we're wasting time sitting around here."

"You got a one track mind, Bugsy," Sniffer chuckled.

"Yeah man, but it's the only track worth following."

There were other things that they knew they must speak of, once the raucous edge was off their voices.

"How's the leg?" Bugsy eventually asked.

71

"Bit of a scar. Itches sometimes. It was really just a flesh wound."

"Heard it hit an artery."

"Just nicked it. Really, I'm fine."

"Pity," Sniffer mused. "Just a millimetre more and you might have scored a homer."

You laughed, but it wasn't funny. That extra millimetre and you would have been dead before you reached the hospital. Instead, you were ready to be returned to the unit, only slightly worse for wear. But at least you didn't have to lie about it any more.

There were the hurried letters home to assure family and friends that you had survived—the panicky newspaper reports you had seen made the facts look relatively tame. Then you had lied, just a scratch from a twig, not even a wound to speak of. You carried a piece of metal that looked like a squashed and shredded sixpence, added to your dogtags on the cord around your neck.

"Alby didn't make it," Sniffer said quietly.

"Never regained consciousness," you could confirm. "I thought he was going to be okay but he was dead in the chopper."

"Poor bastard," Bugsy mused. "Musta pissed him right off knowin' the last thing he ever saw was your smiling face, Yogi."

"Yeah," and you needed to think, to strive to find what little you could feel for Alby Dunshea. "Y'know, I always hated the guy. Despised him. But somehow, now he's dead, I wish I'd known him better."

"You woulda liked him even less, Yogi. He was a flatout arsehole," Bugsy said coldly. It shocked you. Though you might have agreed, Alby was one of your own. And he was dead. The truth was you didn't know how to feel about it, since your emotions had nothing genuine to offer and your intellect didn't care.

"Well," Sniffer chuckled. "The world will be a much prettier place now that his ugly puss won't be around any more."

The joke freed you from thinking things that were better not thought. The saddest thing was that was probably the last time anyone thought much about Alby Dunshea.

"Okay, so, where's the sheilas?" Bugsy demanded.

"Everywhere," you grinned. "And the jack rating is around 95%."

"I'm willing to risk it."

"If you do, next time you have a piss your prick will come off in your hand."

You took them to a nearby bath-house for sauna and massage, so called. Softened by the incense and steam, you drifted to such an extent that when the girl jerked you off, you hardly even noticed. And that after all your warnings to the others to save it for later. Then you took them to a bar where you knew the prices weren't quite as outrageous as most places.

"If you stick to the beer," you warned. "And don't, under any circumstances, buy the girl a Saigon Tea, no matter how convincingly she pleads."

"What's so special about Saigon Tea?"

"It's a thimbleful of warm water at two bucks a throw."

"Thieving hounds."

"Exactly. But you will find that once you've downed a few scotch and drys and the little lovely with her boobs pressed up under her chin has been playing with your prick for a while, the urge to give her the one thing in the world she desires, namely a Saigon Tea, is rather difficult to overcome."

"And how, wise leader, do we meet this hideous threat?"

"We keep moving from bar to bar. By the time the little sweeties realise all their coaxing is to no avail, you've had a hard drink and a nice feel and on we go to the next one."

It worked for a while as well. They dappled in various women without succumbing to a single Saigon Tea and generally managed to avoid all other ways of being ripped off as well.

"Gotta hand it to yer, Yogi," Bugsy laughed. "You sure know how to handle these slopeheads."

But by late afternoon, your leg began to stiffen and all three were drunk and tired and you finally bogged down in a bar named Honolulu and began allowing the time-honoured traditions of the local culture to overwhelm you. The girls seemed nicer than average, the booze less heavily watered down and anyway, you had given them a good run for their money.

"You buy me Saigon Tea, Uc Dai Loi, and I make you wery happy."

"Yeah, sure, Brighteyes, but only one."

"Okay, uney, only one."

They deteriorated swiftly once they had stopped. Sniffer was soon going to sleep and the girl he had contracted had to keep prodding him to produce his wallet. You seemed to be failing to describe to the young thing on your knee exactly what a kangaroo was. Perhaps they had been doped, or was it merely the unfamiliar softness of womankind.

Bugsy, on the other hand, seemed to be descending into belligerence. He sprawled on the chair and brushed aside the girl in a minimal green dress who had been holding his attention for almost an hour.

"You buy me nother," she persisted.

"Go buy your own, you greedy bitch," Bugsy growled.

The girl tried not to understand him.

"You buy me nother Saigon Tea, Uc Dai Loi. You number one. You buy me nother."

Bugsy swept her away again.

"Gowan, piss orf."

With his ruffled hair and day's stubble, Bugsy looked ferocious indeed, but still the girl managed somehow to decide that he was only teasing her. She pushed herself toward him, smiling sweetly.

"Oh baby, uney. Wassa matter?"

Bugsy grabbed her by the throat and heaved her across the room— she landed on her backside with a thump. She immediately sprang to her feet and began to remonstrate angrily, in which she was joined by an older woman in black pyjamas who bulged very severely at the middle. When the older woman opened her mouth, everything was red with the cherryroot she chewed. It seemed to add heat to her fierce unintelligible words. No teeth nor tongue nor any other feature was discernible, but merely a pulsating red hole of fury. So vociferous was the tirade that it woke up Sniffer Gibson.

"What's going on?" he wondered.

"Once more we seem to be losing hearts and minds."

While the woman and the girl continued to voice protest, some sinewy men started to appear in the background, and you decided it was time to be moving on. You grabbed Sniffer and Bugsy by their respective sleeves and dragged and they came along but as Bugsy passed the older woman, she spat, or spluttered possibly, with the result that a blob of the hideous red muck appeared on Bugsy's shirt like a bulletwound.

"You bitch!" Bugsy thundered, and swiped at her.

A small crowd was gathering, joining in the chorus of protest, to which Bugsy rose to his fullest height and let out a roar that would have impressed any randy lioness. It impressed the crowd too, who backed off five paces and fell silent for a moment. Sniffer loved it, bursting into laughter that you tried to share, but immediately the crowd regrouped and resumed their abuse. Bugsy roared again, this time charging a few paces toward them and so created a panic when they all fell over each other as they backed off.

"Dirty foul-smelling little bastards," he seethed as he marched back and the three invaders turned to the door. There, a tighter band of the small men was jammed.

"Oops," Sniffer Gibson said.

But Bugsy was fighting mad and undeterred. He strode straight at them, reaching like a giant amongst dwarfs and, seizing one of the most vocal by the shirt, propelled him backwards into his supporters. The result was that the path to the doorway was cleared as the defenders tumbled out into the street. But when you stepped to the doorway, you immediately saw it was a trap. The crowd surged back, blocking every escape, and directly ahead, a young man stood on the pavement brandishing a very large knife.

Bugsy responded without hesitation, picking up a wooden table and hurling it at his antagonist. The crowd shrieked again and backed off once more, clearing enough space to allow them a beach-head on the footpath. But Bugsy wasn't finished in the bar yet—he emerged with another table that he thrashed several times on the concrete before inverting it and using his foot to detach a leg. Swung to hand, it made a formidable club.

The street was full of people, all chattering and whining loudly in their sing-song voices. Wielding his waddy, Bugsy forced them back until it was clear to the middle of the road and you and Sniffer took up your places behind him.

"They tore me bloody shirt," Sniffer muttered in disgust.

Now the crowd encircled them, forming what might have been a cock-fighting arena. But they were keeping back, out of range of Bugsy and his waddy.

"Which way?" Bugsy asked through gritted teeth.

"I think there's a Yank MP post down this way somewhere," you said uncertainly. For sure, it was too far to go back, toward the billet.

"Do you think we'll make it?" Sniffer asked dubiously.

"I didn't think we'd get this far," you replied grimly.

But you found you were allowed to move in the direction you had indicated, the pliable mob oozing around as you went until everyone was at your back and the street before you was completely deserted. Bugsy walked to the fore, beating the rhythm of the march with the waddy on his hand, while you and Sniffer took up wide positions either side. Like the bad guys in a western, you walked the street with the very vocal crowd accumulating behind—you could only hope that the plan was to escort you from the vicinity.

All along the street, people were hiding in their shops until you passed and then emerging, swelling the crowd behind. Every few paces, Bugsy would stop and raise the waddy menacingly and the crowd would try to halt but those at the back pushed those before them forward, often into the range of Bugsy's arc.

"Keep moving," you shouted at him.

But Bugsy persisted in stopping and flourishing his club, creating chaos in the mob whose voices rose to a frenzy.

Several times, people were thrust too far forward and might have been tempted into making an assault. You rushed at them a couple of paces, roaring furiously as Bugsy had done, and they hurled themselves back against the wall of the oncoming mob in terror.

You had to admit it was great—the sense of power you had over all these people, merely at the sound of your voice. Inside you, hatred of the Vietnamese, their country and everything it stood for welled amidst the alcohol and that sensation of power and control began to overwhelm you. You saw some people waiting in ambush in a fruit shop ahead and charged them, roaring, in fine imitation of a rhino. The people threw up their arms and fled screaming out the back of the shop. You returned to the street, chest-swelled, ferocious, seething with race hatred bred in a year of indoctrination.

So the rampage continued, Bugsy terrorising the mob behind, you and Sniffer by turns roaring and rushing those lurking ahead. You could feel the fear you engendered, all of your apprehension and discomfort had gone now and you were the predator, roaring and thundering, stalking terrified prey, no longer capable of speech nor rational thought. You were your basic, original, animal self, without any of the bullshit that had kept you tamed all your life. Now you had broken out, and never had you so completely felt at one with yourself. The exhilaration was intoxicating. The sheer power and strength of naked unarmed hunter-killer, the terror of the jungle. Your instincts, for just those few moments, had finally completely overcome the years of civilised conditioning. This was who you really were, hunter-killer, master of the earth, the most dangerous predatory animal that ever lived.

And then the moment passed and with it the exhilaration, to be replaced instead by a numb dullness, silent and desperate. On the road ahead, a white landrover had parked, blocking the roadway. Three men climbed out in their white calico uniforms, small Vietnamese policemen—the notorious White Mice. They stood defiantly, barricading the road.

"Us or them?" Bugsy called.

"Them. Definitely," you shouted back.

As if to confirm your assessment, the three White Mice each drew their revolvers.

Now you were trapped. Continue forward and the three armed men might consider themselves attacked, stop and you risked being grabbed or trampled by the mob behind. You looked at the indifference on the faces of the three men and it gave no sign of their intentions.

"Bloody MP's," Bugsy muttered. "Never around when you fucking want them."

"*Dung Lai!*" one of the White Mice bellowed, holding his revolver aloft and, as ordered, everyone stopped. You were about ten metres away from them and the crowd the same distance behind. And all voices were silent now.

"Just look friendly," you said.

Sniffer looked his friendliest.

One of the White Mice, the leader if the embellishments on his uniform were any guide, began making utterances in sing-song Vietnamese that made no sense at all until he motioned with his revolver toward Bugsy's right hand. Bugsy did a dumb act, pointing at the club; the policeman nodded; Bugsy looked blank and shrugged; the policeman repeated his commands more loudly. Bugsy smiled and half-turning, raised the club once more to the crowd. They gasped and cowered.

At that same instant, further down the street behind the White Mice, there was a squeal of tortured tyres and a US Army jeep darted into view, bearing four US MPs.

"Here comes the cavalry," Sniffer grinned.

But you were watching Bugsy who was so caught up in his final moments of neanderthal existence that he could not let it go. He stood, again brandishing the club over his head and again the crowd cowered and the policeman bellowed his commands. Then Bugsy threw it away. He discarded the club into the gutter and turned back toward the policemen with a wildly defiant look. The MPs in the jeep were yelling and blasting on their horn, the policemen were bellowing commands, the crowd were shrieking with anger and Bugsy was roaring in primal fury, and then suddenly it was as if all these sounds were gathered and drawn together into one single louder, sharper, greater sound that absorbed and obliterated them all. In the next instant there was only the report of the revolver, echoing away amid the tall buildings.

Bugsy went sideways as if in pursuit of his discarded club but he only made a few staggering paces before he stumbled and went over sideways, hitting the roadway and sliding into the gutter. His teeth were fiercely gritted, you saw, and his hands seemed to be trying to hold the top of his brow in place. Then the blood exploded between his fingers and he stretched out and his whole body convulsed violently while the blood gushed into the gutter.

The jeep screeched to a halt, three of its occupants deploying while a third stepped up onto the bonnet, aiming his carbine straight at you. A second grabbed Sniffer as he attempted to rush to Bugsy's aid and gripped him around the neck. The third covered the White Mice, the fourth the street.

"Stay where you are, sonny," the man up on the jeep shouted. "Lessen you wanna end up like your friend here."

You stood with your hands at your side, no longer capable of direct movement anyway. Sniffer was wrestled to the ground and then the White Mice holstered their revolvers and climbed into their landrover and drove away. Bugsy had finally come to rest with his back turned, a small spout of blood bubbling up from within his hair and running in tributaries between the corrugations of the roadway. A negro MP stood over Bugsy, shaking his head.

"You guys. You guys. You never learn," he murmured.

Otherwise, the street was completely deserted.

7. Turnover

Operation Tumbarumba—sounds like a belly ache and that's what you've got. The platoon has stopped for lunch, back there in the greenshit, after four days of futile thrashing about in a place where no one has ever been, but there's this track. No footprints or other signs. Not worth an ambush. But you get stuck out here on picket, covering their arses and starving to death. Picket. Silent watching. No eating. No smoking. Alone. An hour of solid self-deprivation.

You're propped in behind the root of a big kapok, and the track runs away downhill in a remarkably straight line for about a hundred metres—an enormous distance to be able to see in this part of the world: far enough for it to disappear in a misty haze that hovers ghostlike in this rain forest country. There are no sounds. There is nothing but you, constantly talking yourself out of lighting a dangerous fag.

Alby Dunshea was dead but everyone hated him and no one cared. Bugsy Norris was dead but everyone loved him and no one cared. You tried to care but every time your thought about him it immediately converted into hatred and thoughts of vengeance on the Vietnamese. All you could do was share in the jokes.

"Pretty good shot to hit someone like Bugsy in the brain."

"If that's the soft option, what's the hard one?"

If they were jokes.

Before long, it was as if he had never been one of them, as if he had never existed at all. At least he had volunteered so it was his own silly fuckin' fault. Hoo Roo Bugsy. Hoo Roo Bogface. The only real effect was that it made you feel luckier to have survived.

There were times, though, deep in the night, when a weird surge of emotion rose unexpectedly in your body and forced tears into your eyes. You fought such weak moments and suppressed them before anyone noticed. Fortunately, they only happened when you were alone and allowed your mind to drift. Like now...

Fuck you, Bugsy. Think about yourself. There's a fuckin' great scar on your calf muscle that itches a lot and the muscle itself has a hollow and has wasted somewhat—you limp when you get tired, which is just about all the fuckin' time. Wounded war hero—what a fuckin' joke. All it did was scare the living daylights out of Wally and Ella when the telegram arrived.

You returned expecting a hero's welcome, but no one seemed to notice. You were one of the last wounded men to be returned to the unit—they all thought you got a homer, but you only went as far as Saigon. Thirty other men had preceded you back to Delta Company, showing off their scars and telling all the hospital horror stories. There was nothing left for you.

And anyway, they were preparing for their first operation since the battle and when you arrived there was a strange air of apprehension about the place. What had once been routine was now an anxiety and no one wanted to talk much, especially about getting wounded.

"I bet I'm happier to see you than you are to see me," Nigel said by way of welcome.

He offered to leave you on the rear party but you had already rested too much.

Greyman handed you the AK.

"I was just keeping it for yer," he grinned.

"Yeah, I bet."

Reinforcements have finally arrived, two new conscripts. Daytripper, whose real name you never learn, is another whingeing Pom except maybe he's got a right to because he came to Aussie on a tourist visa, overstayed and ended up drafted, poor blighter, as he puts it; and a quiet little guy named Mickey Wright who you don't know anything about because you haven't had a chance to talk to him yet.

Everything was the same and yet everything was different. When next morning you flew out into this apparently safe region, these men who once sat recklessly on the landing struts of the choppers and hung out the sides boldly and shiacked each other dangerously now cringed inwardly toward the centre; a tight little huddle of men, contracting more each time the chopper banked, clinging to one another with a shameless intimacy that had never been there before.

"It's as if we've collectively lost our nerve," Sniffer muttered when the nerve-wracking ride was gladly over.

"Maybe we've finally realised this war business is fucking serious," Snowy remarked.

Big black soldier ants march along the ridge of the kapok root. These are the sort that can bore straight through tin cans—they always go straight, through anything, and bite like fuck too. You watch them pass within an inch of your arm with morbid fascination, but they never move off the line. Over trained snappy little bastards. If you don't do something, take some risk, you'll fall asleep. If you do those little fuckers will bore a hole straight through your skull. That keeps you awake...

It all feels strangely insecure with the tight-knit original group now broken. The two new boys stick together, as do the six old hands, but that will sort itself out. A few shots in your general direction makes an old hand of anyone.

Then you are suddenly peering down the track. You don't know why. You just are. Ants forgotten. Fag forgotten. You tighten your grip on the AK. You are peering right down to the end of the track, as far as you can see, into the murk of the haze. Wait. Wait. Something moves.

Impossible to say what it is. Just a fleeting glimpse of movement, and some sort of specific sounds and rustles amid the faint background cacophony of the forest, but it was something, rather than nothing. You wait and watch, eyes wanting to be zeroed in on the exact spot. There he goes! A man, or the silhouette of one, passes through your perception in one tiny instant and then is gone, as if it never was, only it was. Now you know where and what. Wait on it. Few more seconds. Wait. Wait. There he goes. Another figure briefly glimpsed only this time you've seen black clothing, a rifle held level, the curved magazine of an AK47, just like the one you carry. Charlies!

Waiting, waiting, watching, watching, but that's it. The sound has stopped. They have stopped. Down there, by the track. Nothing else happens. You might have imagined it, so completely has any trace of it passed. Might have nodded off and dreamed it. Like fuck you have!

Hold on a moment. Think it through. Get the fuckin' story straight before you go creating a panic. No immediate dangers. They're a hundred metres away and going nowhere. Crossing the track from left to right. Four of them. And there was something else. Something nags. Let it go. It'll come. Four of them. The first caught your attention; were there more before you detected him? No, not a chance. You picked the signs clearly. He had to be the first. The second zeroed you in on the spot; or was it the first man seen twice? No again—there was a definite pause between your apprehension of the one and the other. Two men. You glimpsed the third; no doubt about that, and then saw the fourth with his AK. Or was it an AK? That's what nags. Looked a little bit large in proportion to the figure. Maybe a larger, similar weapon, there's a Chinese Bren Gun with a curved mag under. Might be one of those... Stopped by the track. One hundred metres down. Okay. That's it. All you know about it. Here we go.

Slowly, quietly, you haul yourself to your feet. Your leg is cramped and has gone to sleep—silly fucking thing. Silly fucking you for not keeping your limbs nimble, that is. You go real careful, real quiet. Reasonable to assume that if you could hear them, they can hear you. You head back quietly, in no hurry, toward the platoon. Spargo's there, sitting by the gun, eating those Ham and Lima beans that no one else can stomach. He looks up and sees you standing there, twenty metres away. You give the thumbs down, and the signal goes through the camp in a matter of seconds.

You drop down beside Snowy, wave Sniffer over, and light a cigarette while he approaches. That one fag a day that you really need. Sniffer was out there on picket earlier—you relieved him, so he knows the terrain.

"There's four Charlies down the track, bottom of the hill. They stopped there. Out of sight."

No further explanation needed. Sniffer nods and heads off to take up your position at the picket post, while you sort this out.

In moments, Nigel and Holly are there with puzzled looks. You repeat the statement, edited for their benefit.

"Four Charlies. Armed. Hundred metres down the track. Stopped on the right side."

Holly sees it as his job to doubt everything.

"You sure there's four?"

"Certain."

"Hundred metres. Long way. You sure they're Charlies."

"Weapon with curved mag. AK47 maybe."

"You carry an AK, Yogi."

"They were small."

"Stopped, you say."

"Came in left to right across the track and went no further."

"Ambush," Nigel said flatly.

"You think they know we're here, Yogi."

"You bet. I reckon they're waiting in ambush for us down there."

Holly sighs. Life is a worry to great doubters.

"We have assurances from SAS and the Yanks that there are no Charlies in the area."

"They're wrong."

But he moves back to his radio man and speaks to higher authorities. He asks around. Does any unit have men in this area?

"What's he fuckin' pissin' around for?" Snowy Spargo complains. "Why don't we just go down and get 'em, while they're still there."

No one answers. Best to play it safe. And if they are lying in ambush, they'll wait for you to get there, just like you would.

"No friendlies around," Holly says. "So you may be right, Yogi."

Maybe... No one dignifies that with an answer either.

"How many weapons did you see?"

"Just one. Others were indistinct. And the one seemed too large for an AK47."

"Bigger, similar weapon, you mean?" Nigel asks. It's best to know what you are up against.

"Yeah, maybe," but there is a doubt there. What's wrong with this? You don't believe your answer now. Still it nags.

"Or a very small man," Nigel proposes.

"Or else you've got the distance wrong, Yogi," Holly pipes in. "And they were further away than you thought."

"No. Distance is right."

Holly deliberates. What he deliberates is obvious, and finally he realises that.

"You want to take them, Nigel?"

"Sure."

"Heavy weapon in ambush. Very tricky."

"We can handle it."

"You'll be relying on Yogi's guesswork."

"If Yogi says that's what's there, then that's what's there."

You spend the next few minutes getting your suddenly inflated ego back under control.

But Holly continues to fret. "He might have imagined it."

"He might not have too. We're wasting time. Let's go."

"I'll move the rest of the platoon over to the track as back up. You happy to walk your blokes into this?"

The spider is in its web and the little fly leader says 'Head for the centre.' And he asks if we're happy...

"Yep," Nigel says with false confidence.

"Okay, let's go."

You don't wait for the platoon. You move straight out onto the track. No one needs to say anything. This all depends on you having got it right, but it's best not to think too deeply about that. Just get on with the job. You go to pick up Sniffer at the picket post.

"See anything?"

Sniffer shakes his head.

"Lead it, Yogi."

This time Sniffer doesn't complain about surrendering his forward scout role; it's your hand and you have to play it. You will lead them

85

down the track and get as close as you dare, then point to the spot where the ambush is placed and you blow the shitbags out of it. Simple. Unless you go a few paces too far, walk into the trap, and wear it. You lead, and Snowy follows with the M60. Usually Nigel, navigating, comes second, but now you want the firepower up front. Your biggest problem will be getting out of Snowy's way, and you've buggered that up in the past. Then comes Nigel, Sniffer with Daytripper and Mickey Wright tucked safely down the back. They'll run the flank if they know how—Nigel patiently explains what that means.

"When it starts, we wheel right, into the jay and then go straight down through 'em."

And bloody Greyman's in Bangkok rooting himself silly, lucky bastard. A Bangkok smile passes glowingly through your memory and your whole body tingles for a delicious moment... Keep your fuckin' mind on the job, you dickhead!

You start down the track. There is the place they went in, and just ahead of it a sapling leans out onto the track. That's the spot you're heading for. You go easy, careful with each step, watching and listening all the while. You don't look back but you can sense them behind you. Snowy right on your heels—you can hear him breathe—then a gap to Nigel, another gap to the other three.

It seems to take forever. That sapling is a light year away. Time has slowed down again, even before the shooting starts. You want to run down there and get it over with, but you gotta play the game. One step, then the next, eyes fixed on the place where they went down, ears stretching on the sides of your head such that you can actually feel them. There isn't a sound. There's nothing to work with. Just a memory to guide you which, as the man said, you might have imagined, or got wrong. But you can't afford to think wrong now. The sapling is five paces away and ten paces beyond that the track turns sharply left. You didn't think of that. They came up the track, not across it, and set the ambush at the corner—the best possible place. An ambush works better if you can hit 'em head on. Now that you are down here, nothing looks the way it did when you saw it from a distance. It's all wrong, you are sure. They might be to the right—smarter if they were straight ahead. You can't tell. But they went right. You said they went right. They went right.

Three paces to the sapling. It's not close enough to the corner. You need three, maybe four, more paces, before you hit the right spot. Or will that be too many? They are in there, pointing their weapons at you, waiting, ready to mow you down. How many more paces are they waiting for? You reach the sapling, and stop. No, stick to the original plan. This is where you thought it was. This is where it is. Here. Do it now!

You look back at the men behind you. All eyes are on you as they stand there, tense, intent. You turn and point to the place at the right and then dive away to the left.

Snowy opens up with a long murderous burst, standing right in the middle of the track like the Colossus of Rhodes, firing from the hip. The area of jungle you indicated explodes in a fury of flying dirt and leaves and splinters as you hit the ground on the far side of the track, roll and bring the AK around to bear. Snowy is spraying the whole area but you must look for a specific target, as Sniffer, hanging back with the rocket, waiting to see the right spot to hit. The other three have gone right, straight into the jungle where they will come charging down three abreast, hitting them on the flank. Nigel, directing traffic.

"Go, you blokes, go! Hit 'em hard! Come on, Sniffer, fire that fucking rocket!"

Look for something, anything! And it's there! Muzzle flashes in through the scrub. You fire straight at them. Something hits the dirt on the track beside you and dances brilliantly as it does a dazzling momentary back flip before your eyes. Tracers. They're firing back, the bastards! You rip off a mag into the spot those flashes came from and then do a quick change. Then there is a double crunch—deafening: Sniffer has seen the tracers too and lets them have it with the rocket. Everything then is lost in smoke, as you eardrums scream in painful protest.

Now Snowy seizes the chance to drop flat on the track, ready to fire from the prone position, and Nigel is going wide, bent double, hunting some cover. Deeper in you hear the flankers blazing away as they descend, but that's all, that's all. No one is firing back now. Zero incoming.

"Hold your fire, hold it! Stop where you are!" Nigel is shouting.

It stops. The gunfire echoes away, sounding like other, more distant battles, far off in the jungle. You wait. There is a sound. It is a sort of whimpering noise, like a dog left on a chain. In there. A tremor of joy runs through your body. They were there, where you said they were. You picked the spot, dead on. Got it right. You fuckin' balltearer! You'll be a living legend around Nui Dat for this and everyone will want to buy you a beer. Yogi Bear, who turned over a Viet Cong ambush. What a fuckin' hero!

"You okay, Yogi?"

"No worries, Nige."

"Snowy, how's the gun."

"Red hot, Nigel."

"Daytripper?"

"I got killed but I died game."

"Dickhead. Sniffer?"

"Two Charlies down right in front of me, Nigel."

"Okay. And the other bloke...what's your fuckin' name?"

"Mickey Wright, sir..."

"Don't fuckin' call me sir you moron. Just tell me whether or not you're fuckin' dead."

"I'm not dead, Corporal."

"Dead right, Wright. Sniffer's got two Charlies down. Anyone else got anything?"

"There seems to be a bit of a clearing there, Nigel," Daytripper was saying. "And they were all in there. Nothing moving now. But someone's alive. I can hear them."

There is that pathetic whimper, softer now.

"Want to have a look, Yogi?"

Oh shit!

"Haven't I done enough?"

"You're having a big day, Yogi. Might as well wrap it up proper."

"Yeah, sure."

"Daytripper says one of them is still alive."

"Yeah, I can hear it."

"We'll give 'em another burst if you like."

"No. I'll have a look."

"Hold your fire, boys. Yogi Bear's having a look."

"Good old Yogi."

You are about to move, when suddenly a voice can be heard way up the track. Holly. "What's going on down there, Nigel?"

"Shut up. We're busy."

But in the moment of distraction, something happens for which your senses cannot account. Suddenly, there is someone standing on the track before you. All of your reflexes spring to level the AK and blow the living daylights out of the figure, but nothing like that happens. What you see is too arresting, too horrifying, for that.

She is ten or eleven years old and stands in a trance at the edge of the track, staring vacantly into space with her huge child's eyes. She is completely naked—perhaps the blast from the rocket had stripped away her clothing—although she does seem to be wearing a red cloak cast over her right shoulder and running down to her knee. But it isn't a cloak, it is a great stream of blood, gushing from a wound high on her chest. It is from her that the whimpering sound is emitting.

For a moment, you just stare, and she stares right back at you with those great eyes pleading with the world for pity, for help.

"Good God," you hear Snowy breathe, and his face falls into his hands.

You cannot accept what you are seeing. In utter disbelief, you stand and walk over, all notions of safety and security abandoned now, and as you approach those eyes lock upon yours and follow until she is looking up at you pleadingly when you stand beside her. What have you done to me, they seem to be asking in her child's innocence. You are reaching out to touch her, perhaps wanting to assure yourself that she is real, has substance, but the very moment your fingers contact her arm, she collapses as if you have unsettled the

89

faint equilibrium that held her there. Like a house of cards in the breeze, she drops at your feet and flops about there like a landed fish and you stand, powerless to move.

"What's happening?" Nigel asks, for he can tell it has all gone horribly wrong.

"A kid...she's just a bloody kid..."

"What?" Nigel cries uncomprehending.

But then comes the awful pronouncement from Sniffer who has done some investigating of his own. "There's three more of them in here."

By then you were on your knees and raised her to a sitting position, her head lolling against your shoulder. All the light seemed to have gone from those eyes. They no longer riveted you with accusation. Nigel stepped onto the track, shaking his head, quivering in horror.

"Holly! Holly! Get the fuckin' medic down here. Now!"

There was nothing Ten Days could do. The girl had died of shock the moment that you touched her. In the small clearing was a boy of eight with his face completely blown off, and two more youths of about thirteen, shot to pieces. The platoon came down and took over, while each of you moved away, trying to find a place where the world made some sort of sense. There was no such place.

"Kids. They're just kids," Snowy was murmuring, over and over, as he wandered around on the track. Mabel, a love betrayed, is abandoned forever. And nearby Sniffer lay flat on his back in the middle of the track, staring up at the canopy above.

"No one touch me. Don't anyone come near me."

You don't know what happened to the others, and at the time you didn't care. You went down the track a way and found a log to sit on. You didn't bother to take the abandoned AK along with you—if someone came and killed you, that was probably just as well. By the time you'd smoked three cigarettes, Nigel came down and brought the AK.

"It wasn't your fault, Yogi."

"Oh no? I said they were small. Remember? I said they were fuckin' small, didn't I."

"You couldn't have known."

"But I did know! I knew it was wrong! Too small, I said. I just didn't think about it enough."

"No one could have thought of that."

"It's wrong, Nigel. We did not come here to kill children."

"They were Viet Cong children."

"They were just fuckin' kids!"

"We were doing the job the government pays us for."

"If the government pays us to kill children, then it has to be wrong."

"Yogi, they were armed. They were lying in ambush for us. They fired back. If you hadn't sprung 'em, they'd have wiped us out, just like their mums and dads would have."

"Are you seriously trying to justify this?"

Your shrill outburst causes him to draw breath. Placatingly, he tries again. "What about their parents? Don't you think they bear some responsibility for their kids..."

"Nigel, when I was a kid, I used to play games with guns. Cowboys and indians, gangsters, wargames. Sometimes I'd pinch me old man's shotgun and go out and play Great White Hunters. Nobody came along and shot the shitbags outa me for that."

"Yogi, these people are into total war. They train their children for it. You don't understand how primitive they are..."

"Maybe. But we are supposed to be civilised human beings. And civilised human beings don't gun down children. Not for any reason."

"Don't do this to yourself, Yogi. It wasn't your fault."

"Words, Nigel. Just fuckin' words."

You walked away, again leaving the AK behind. They say that Nigel sat on the log and wept, but you don't know whether that was true. You had to do something. Words were nothing. What you did counted. You went across to where Kinross's blokes were digging. You walked right up to them and shoved them all out of the way, then grabbed an entrenching tool and held it aloft, menacing anyone who tried to come near.

"I'm doing this," you snarled.

You dug the hole good and deep and square, while the other men looked on. From time to time, one or another would offer to relieve you and you didn't answer. You just dug.

"Right, bring them over."

Bulldog Doyle carried the girl and Ten Days the boy. The two youths were apparently being put in a hole somewhere else. They laid the two small corpses beside the hole in which you still stood in your mad defiance.

"Why aren't you blokes helping him?" Doyle asked.

"You try and get near him," Kinross said.

"Come on, Yogi. Get out of there."

"Piss off, Bulldog."

"That's an order, Griffin."

"Stick it up your arse."

His bulldog tactics failed, Doyle tried a gentler tone.

"Hey, Griffin. Come on. Let someone else do this bit."

"Get away," you growled at him.

"Yogi, we're getting a chopper to take you and the others out. Give it to someone else."

"Don't come near me or you'll wear this."

"You'll miss the fucking chopper."

"Fuck the fuckin' chopper."

"Alright Griffin. Get on with it."

"Let's get them in the hole, shall we?"

At least someone had closed the girl's big eyes, and the boy was turned mercifully face down. Lying in the damp red soil, the girl's naked body was so appallingly white.

"At least someone could have spared a fuckin' hoochie," you savaged at them. Quite a crowd had gathered and no one moved. You stripped off your shirt and draped it over her.

First the girl, then the boy. You laid them carefully, gently, in the bottom of the hole and then climbed out and began to fill it in. You shovelled furiously, heaping the dirt onto any part of their bodies still exposed but somehow it seemed that no matter how much dirt you hurled in there, some part of them still remained exposed. A tiny white hand, part of a foot, and more than thirty years later you're still shovelling and you haven't quite managed to cover them yet.

8. Pumpkins

Next there's a flying cow. Fair fuckin' dinkum, a real cow, about fifty feet above the ground, going moo madly, swinging helplessly in the air. All it needed was the fuckin' moon for it to sail over... but this is no nursery rhyme. The poor bloody animal was suspended in a giant sling connected to the belly of a hovering Chinook with US Air Force markings, oscillating wildly in the gusty air.

"Poor cow," you said sadly.

The cow would trapeze its bovine way across the treetops for three kilometres to where a convoy of trucks waited, guarded by Armoured Corp. That was as close as they could get to this village; it was all narrow muddy jungle tracks from there on to here. The village, without benefit of a name, has a population of a few dozen but a vast storage of produce and area of crops. Far too fuckin' vast. It's a Charlie supply base, no fuckin' worries about that.

But the villagers aren't Charlies. They're just plain folks whose hamlet is under the Charlie's thumb—keep up the supply of food or you get a bullet in the brain. Nice and simple. Even dumb peasant dirt farmers understand it perfectly.

So all the stock and equipment gets lifted out by choppers, and the people are rounded up but they have to walk out to the trucks, escorted by Ten Platoon. They'll be rehoused in what is called the Engineer's Village, built by the Sappers near Nui Dat, surrounded by barbed wire and guarded by MP's so the Charlie's can't get at them. No one is allowed to call it a concentration camp.

Twelve platoon has thrown a perimeter around this hamlet in case any Charlie patrols get hungry at this inconvenient time, and you're in the middle to do the rest—burn the houses and wreck the crops.

94

Search and destroy operation. Nice day's work in sunny Vietnam.

"Picture this, Snowy," you are saying, now that the cow has passed from view. "You are sitting on the verandah of your farm out west there, the wife in the kitchen, kids playing in the yard. Then a bunch of soldiers come along, round up you and your family and march them off to a concentration camp, steal your stock, burn your house down, wreck your crops. How would you feel about that?"

"You think too much, Yogi," Snowy grumbles.

"You reckon there's any way you could be convinced that them fuckin' soldiers were doing you a favour?"

"Yogi Bear, what are you fuckin' on about?"

"This! I'm on about this! I've seen movies. John Wayne movies. Richard Attenborough movies. There's the way the good guys behave and then there's the way the Rotten Nazis and Dirty Japs behave. And this? This relocating populations, burning farms, destroying crops. It's the way the bad guys carry on."

"Which only proves you watch too many movies, Yogi."

"But don't you see, Snowy? Don't you see?"

"Yogi, will you piss off and earbash someone else for a while. You're giving me the shits."

Snowy Spargo just wasn't any fun since he broke up with Mabel. He has simply refused to carry her any further, and declared himself an ordinary rifleman. You all had to go down to the firing range and be tested for your M60 skills. You were good and big and strong enough but Nigel had made you his 2IC in place of Alby Dunshea. The only other possibility was Daytripper who wasn't so big but he has a lot of gumption, so he got the job. Meanwhile, Snowy watched grumpily and refused even to join the practice. Back in the middle with an SLR, he somehow looks smaller, less significant, and anyway is constantly in a black mood. Every morning, first time you see him, he tells you how many days he has to go. You and Greyman and Sniffer have the same number of days and everyone keeps count, but he tells you anyway. He is pissed off with you and everything, but then, so was everyone that day.

There was a Thanksgiving party going on at Bein Hoa base and the Yankee pilots didn't appreciate being dragged out to give Delta Company a ride to this hamlet. They fumbled their choppers maniacally, playing chicken with each other, wandering all over the sky in no formation whatsoever, and landed right in the middle of the hamlet with guns blazing into the surrounding jungle, and tumbled you out with your shattered nerves.

"This is stupid, Nigel. Why fuckin' destroy the place? Why not set ambushes on all the tracks and wait until the Charlies come in to try and collect their supplies."

"This is easier."

"But stupid."

"Since when did you expect better than stupid from Task Force."

Soon the people were gone and the cattle and goats with them and all that remained was a friendly-looking dog on a chain.

"Here, doggy. Nice doggy. Come on, boy," Nigel said encouragingly.

The dog bit him and he had to be evacuated for fear of rabies.

This little mishap brought the rage of Hatrack amongst us.

"Bloody bloke his age and rank oughta know bloody better. Did you get rid of the fucking dog?"

"No. It was..." you mumbled, directing a hateful gaze at the departing chopper that carried Nigel away and saw you suddenly promoted into the direct path of Hatrack's tirade.

"Oh Jesus," Hatrack moaned, contorting his craggy face in purest anguish. "Well for Christ's sake shoot the fucking thing before some other fuckwit decides to feed it a finger!"

Only the callous farmboy Snowy Spargo could be persuaded to undertake so foul a duty. You buried the dog at the side of the road with a barbed wire cross at its head and a large old bone at its feet.

Hatrack was soon obliged to return when Mickey Wright and Sniffer discovered the disadvantages of setting fire to a thatched house from the inside. Dorset and Sergeant Lawson rushed to their rescue and the result was four men overcome by smoke and coughing their guts out. Ten Days asked for a chopper to evacuate them, which was why Hatrack exploded once more in your midst, hotter and more redfaced than any of the victims.

"If you cannot control this mob of juvenile delinquents, Mr Hollingsworth, then I will replace you with someone who can!"

While Holly was relaying much the same message to you, Ten Days was silly enough to ask about his dust-off helicopter.

"Fuck the dust-off," Hatrack roared. "Make the stupid bastards walk out!"

The four smoke inhalation victims immediately saw good reason for miraculous recoveries.

Holly led the platoon away from the blazing village, and just over the hill they came upon the most enormous pumpkin patch any of you had ever seen. Truly, it was out of all proportion to the probable needs of the entire Viet Cong army, and although they were the small round Asian pumpkins, still they were plainly very ripe and ready for the harvest.

"Shit, look at 'em all. It's a bloody plague!" Daytripper gasped.

"Today Phouc Tuy, tomorrow, the world," Greyman foretold.

With the fires in the houses now dwindling, it remained only to destroy the pumpkins but so massive did the task appear that Eleven Platoon could only stand along the ridge, gazing in a paralysis of astonished intimidation.

"Bloody good pumpkins too," you were muttering. "Better than the muck we get back at the Dat, if we get any at all."

In the greasy flyblown kitchens of Nui Dat, potato was always mashed, cauliflower similarly; turnips, parsnips and baked custard all had exactly the same texture and taste, carrot was the same stuff coloured red, pumpkin merely dyed with saffron.

Holly, though, faced the vast yellow hoard without compunction, machete raised like a cavalry officer, and ordered in his shrill voice. "Right men! Draw machetes! Charge!!"

The men waded into the field, following their bold leader, slicing and hacking. It was a massacre and more than you could stand.

"This is disgusting. So wasteful."

"Shut up, Yogi Bear, or I'll mistake you for a pumpkin."

"But Jesus, Snowy. It isn't right."

"I've forgotten the last time we did something right," Snowy answered and hacked on.

The platoon moved through in a great sweep, flailing their weapons and those plump round shapes were swiftly reduced to seedy pulp. You strode forth, spying a big healthy specimen and down upon it you swept, slashing a mighty blow, not into the yellowness, but through the stem. Sheathing your machete, you picked up the pumpkin and carried it out of the field to a small flat area beyond, setting it down gently, and then returned to the fray to rescue another. You toiled on, liberating pumpkin after pumpkin, until you had accumulated twenty-six of them, which was exactly the number of men remaining in Eleven Platoon. Except you'd forgotten to count Mickey Wright.

The men now came down the hill, wiping the yellow pulp from the blades and sheathing their machetes. The slaughter was ended.

They came to the place where you stood proudly by your pile of survivors.

"Good on yer, Yogi Bear," Ten Days was laughing. "So what do we do with them. Eat 'em before we go back?"

"How can we, as decent human beings, condone such wastage..." you cried to the mob.

"We ain't decent human beings—we're soldiers," Greyman interjected. But you could ignore the heckling of the rabble.

"Look, at Nui Dat, vegetables are scarce. Take these back with us, and the cooks will go out of their minds."

"So, I reckon, will Hatrack," Dorset observed.

"Oh come on. Even Hatrack will see merit in something like this."

Holly, of course, was looking most distressed about it all. "We should ask him first."

Dorset wasted some time trying to get a radio message through, but the major had already returned to Nui Dat.

"So he probably won't even find out. And if he does, he can't help but approve."

Holly decided to try and point out impracticalities. "Maybe, Griffin. But how do you plan to get these back to Nui Dat. Stuff one in each pocket?"

But of course you had thought of that. "We can put them inside out shirts. Plenty of·space. No trouble at all."

This was true. An army-issue shirt, like an army-issue anything else, was always several sizes too large, and except for Snowy, they all found they could accommodate a pumpkin and still fasten all the buttons.

"Initiative *and* imagination," Sergeant Lawson groaned. "You'll never make an officer, Yogi."

It was such a simple plan, so foolproof, so worthy, so very public-spirited that there could only have been one possible outcome—it had to fail. And the point of failure was, of course, the obvious one, for while it was true that Hatrack had returned prematurely to Nui Dat, it was also true that he had taken up a perfect ambush position at the side of the airstrip. When the choppers carrying Eleven Platoon arrived, the men jubilant and their shirts bulging with the knowledge that something good had been done that day, they disembarked and saw Hatrack standing there and knew it was undone. It was plain from his expression that twenty-six soldiers in an apparent advanced state of pregnancy was by no means what he had been expecting to see. His mouth dropped open like a giant cave in the cliff of his rockhard face, and the dragon in that cave bellowed in just the manner that had achieved for him his wide-spread fame.

"You men! Stop where you are! Lt Hollingsworth! Step forward!"

Eleven Platoon halted in a tight little group on the tarmac, everyone trying to hide behind someone else. Holly wandered forward, striving to look like he was there entirely by mistake.

The only advantage in Holly's position was that he was not carrying a pumpkin himself. Hatrack, in true tactical form, held the high ground and had Holly squinting into the sun, squirming with the knowledge that his earlier roastings were about to be enlarged upon.

"Well, Mr Hollingsworth. Let's hear it!"

"Sir, those are pumpkins. The men are trying to aid the mess situation. What with good vegies being in such short supply..."

But Holly ran out of puff, and anyway was completely drowned out. "Don't give me that, Lieutenant! When I give an order, I expect it to be obeyed!"

"But sir..."

"No buts, Mr Hollingsworth. I'll be talking to you later, understand?"

"Yes sir..."

Holly, helpless, defeated, downcast, wandered aside.

Hatrack now redirected his meanest gaze to the rest of the you, and you strove to meet that gaze with one of equal ferocity.

"Alright, you lot. Pumpkins, is it? Well, let's see them. Come on, out and on the ground in front of you."

You unbuttoned your shirt and lowered the pumpkin to the ground—it was a telling point that most men had already given up hope, opening their shirts to let their pumpkins fall incriminatingly at their feet. You bastard, Hatrack, you breathed, and might have made a charge right there and then, had Snowy not been holding onto your belt from behind.

"Steady, Yogi Bear," he whispered in your ear.

Hatrack came down from the embankment and moved toward you, his eyes blazing, his mouth twisted, jaw jutting ruthlessly. "Right, you pumpkin-eaters. You are going to have to learn something and it is called discipline. Got it? DISCIPLINE! When I give an order, I expect it to be obeyed. I do not expect it to be treated as some sort of joke..."

You lowered your head sadly. The fuckin' rotten smallminded shitheaded bastard. All he fuckin' knows is discipline—the sort of fuckin' mindless discipline that has nothing to do with common sense.

"As it stood," he went on. "had you wanted to keep the pumpkins, all you had to do was ask. That's the system—ASK! I like pumpkin too, you know!"

All eyes turned toward Holly. This was his moment, his chance to explain the efforts made to do just that. But the little runt, standing headbent, was going to let it pass. Fuckin' little gutless freak! Snowy gave an extra jerk on your belt. Tell him, for god's sake, Holly, tell him. But the runt's nerve failed him, and Hatrack carried on regardless. "But no, not you lot. You have to go behind my back, sneaking about like thieves. And that is exactly what's wrong with this outfit. Well you are not going to get away with it this time. You are going to learn..."

And you sagged defeatedly in Snowy's grasp. That was the end—the chance was gone. When Hatrack said someone would learn something, all reason was overwhelmed, no matter what was said or done afterward. "...you are going to learn what discipline is and you will learn it now!..."

Yeah, yeah.

"...Right! Every man, draw his machete! COME ON, GET THEM OUT! NOW! MOVE!"

You knew what it meant—the old put-things-back-the-way-they-were routine, no matter how ridiculous the consequences. Fuckin' army was getting sillier and more childish by the day. Useless fuckin' dickheads, and you whip out your machete like a Saracen warrior about to charge...

"Right!" Hatrack roared. "NOW CUT UP THOSE PUMPKINS!"

Other men stood staring in disbelief, but not you. You only had to glance down at that pumpkin at your feet and it turned into Hatrack's head, with its great nose, sneering lips, cold narrow eyes, jutting lower jaw.

"Come on, you heard me!" Hatrack was bellowing. "DO IT! NOW!"

But you didn't need it spelled out. Hatrack's severed head lay at your feet and you flew to the task. With a cry you lifted your machete aloft and brought it slicing downward to cleave that evil face into two neat halves, and you saw the brain spill out and the blood explode all about. Cop that you bastard Hatrack and struck again and again, slash, slash, slash, and other men, perhaps capturing the same image, began going at it like demons too. Kill Hatrack kill. Die you bastard die!

"GET INTO IT!" Hatrack was screaming in an utter frenzy. "FASTER YOU MEN! SHOW YOU MEAN IT!"

Hatrack, striding back and forth, livid and crazed with the madness of the moment, and the men slashing and slicing furiously, until those pumpkins were chopped to the right size for the cooking pot and then more and more. But with every blow you struck, the divided head of Hatrack became two smaller heads that each need be sliced to two smaller ones, little bloodied heads of Hatrack die you bastard die...

"Alright, STOP!"

And you slashed and slashed at the hundred head hydra of Hatrack, kill, kill, kill them all, slash, slash...

"I SAID STOP, ACTING LANCE-CORPORAL GRIFFIN!"

Snowy shook you and you stopped, panting madly, machete dangling from your hand, your face burning with sweat, glaring straight at your tormentor. Still alive but I'll get you, you bastard. From his high vantage point, Hatrack's face was taunt and his eyes narrow with murderous intent. And the fifty-two eyes that met his gaze were no different.

There was a lull in the fury, and time for more Hatrack speechmaking. "You men are irresponsible and you are also thieves. THIEVES! You are also undisciplined, childish and damned poor soldiers. Good soldiers follow orders unquestioningly. So let's see if you can do it. Ready? Every man, one pace forward—MARCH!"

In perfect drill order, the men stomped one pace forward, which brought them to stand right in the middle of their respective piles of chopped pumpkin. Daytripper slipped over in the goo but nothing could be funny now. You stood exactly in the middle of your mangled yellow pile.

"Right, now...ready for it...Platooooon...Mark TIME!"

You began to march on the spot, grinding pumpkin into the loose gravel at the edge of the airstrip.

"ON THE DOUBLE!"

And you ran and they ran, up and down on the spot, squashing and splattering the orange goo like some idiot tribal ritual, the muck

102

and pulp splotching all over the boots and lower part of the trousers. And the orchestrator of the madness leapt about on his stage and raged and rampaged in accord with his creation.

"FASTER! COME ON, FASTER, YOU THIEVES! GET THOSE KNEES UP! HIGHER! HIGHER, YOU THIEVES, HIGHER!"

The mad wardance continued until the individual puddles of crushed pumpkin became one great one. And Hatrack came down from his high ground to inspect the handiwork.

"Okay, HALT!"

You stood panting, all of you, from the exertion, faces fiery as much from anger as effort. Hatrack advanced to point blank range— easy pumpkin throwing distance were you still armed.

"Good, good. See, you can follow orders after all," he said as if gently scolding a mischievous child. "But look at the mess you've made. We can't go leaving a mess like that all over the airstrip, can we? Of course not. So you'd better pick it all up, hadn't you— every seed and morsel—and since you like carrying pumpkins around inside your shirts, you'll better put it all back where it came from. Got it?"

You didn't get it. It was too unbelievable. But Hatrack could be patient. "I want to be sure you learn that carrying pumpkin around inside your shirts is not such a good idea after all, so PICK THIS FUCKING SHIT UP, YOU THIEVES, AND PUT IT BACK INSIDE YOUR SHIRTS! I WANT THIS AREA LEFT SPOTLESS!"

The men hesitated for one more incredulous moment, and then slowly knelt and began to scoop up the muck in their hands and place it inside their shirts. It oozed horribly in their fingers and quickly stained down the front of their greens. You were the last to kneel, and Hatrack stood, hands on hips, glaring maniacally, until you went down too.

"You will take it back to the company area and there dispose of it in an orderly manner. And you will march back to the area in proper formation. Lt Hollingsworth. CSM Doyle. You will see that this is done. Now get on with it!" And he silenced the murmur of protest with a savage. "And there's no need to talk about it! Your parade, CSM."

It can hardly be supposed that you have ever experienced carrying about ten big serves of uncooked mashed pumpkin pressed coldly against your bare belly by your fastened shirt buttons. It was an exquisitely unpleasant sensation. Every man bent forward slightly, trying to contain the gruesome bundle in his shirtfront, looking like he had just been gutted and was striving to hold his insides in. The shirts bulged with the saggy soggy mess that ran down the thighs, puddling in the crotch and the boots, and soaking clammily through the fabric. It was like wearing back-to-front a nappy that some giant baby had shat in. A rather shamefaced Bulldog Doyle lined you up in three ranks and marched you up the road in a decidedly awkward bandylegged waddling gait.

"Ah, well," Greyman sighed. "Could be worse. I don't like pumpkin much anyway."

"You're on mess duties for a week, Goolie," Holly screeched in exasperation.

"No use crying over spilt pumpkin," Greyman grinned.

"Two weeks!"

The platoon puddled along like a giant snail leaving a yellow sheening trail behind. Holly was thinking about it.

"And a week for you too, Yogi Bear."

"That'll teach me to mess with Viet Cong pumpkins."

"Two weeks!"

It was, however, a very different Lt Hollingsworth who, later that evening, wandered over to the kitchen where Greyman and you were dixie bashing—scrubbing at the hopelessly stained pots and pans burned black by the useless cooks. The rest of the platoon were relieving their embarrassment in the boozer, while the rest of the company, and indeed the entire Task Force, were gurgling mirthfully into their beer. The humiliation of one of the supposedly toughest outfits around was the only subject worth discussing that evening. And this demeanour extended even into the Pig Battalion Officer's Mess, the orderly, white tableclothed impeccable uniformed domain of the high and mighty where, according to Holly, this small scene had just been witnessed.

Porky, the rotund, pompous-looking Battalion Commander, approached Hatrack the moment formalities ended.

"I heard you nearly managed to capture us some nice fresh pumpkins today, Major."

Hatrack, according to Holly, went a most peculiar pale shade. "Not quite, sir."

"Pity. Fancy a spot of pumpkin myself."

To which Hatrack, uncharacteristically, could find no answer.

Before he walked smilingly away, Porky added. "It's good that the rank and file appreciate the critical food shortfalls, don't you think Major? I do hope you'll personally thank the men responsible for today's attempt. You will do that for me, won't you Major."

"Of course I will, sir."

And, of course, he never did.

9.   The Chi-Com Man's Revenge

You are the Chi-Com Man. He lives on in your body as well as your mind—the true hero of Vietnam. No good role for John Wayne here—he's too big and nowhere near subtle enough. More like Peter Lorre, before he bloated and died, but no, too villainous. Someone small and quiet, friendly and brilliant. Humphrey Bogart and Clark Gable and Alan Ladd were all runts but they were photographed to look tall—that's the American way—bigness. They know big, understand it, can match big with bigger, but they know nothing about small. They think small means insignificant and ignore it, and that is their greatest mistake. They don't realise that everything big is made up from things small—ignore the small and the big constantly erodes, fails, falls apart, often inexplicably. Or at least, inexplicably to those who ignore the small. The Chi-Com Man is Charlie Chaplin with a bomb. And it is because they cannot imagine that character that they can never defeat him, for you cannot defeat something you cannot see, and so they watch their empire falling apart, eroded by the invisible for no reason they can comprehend. You are the Chi-Com Man. You can feel yourself diminishing in size, and growing in stature at the same time. You are the Chi-Com Man and the Chi-Com Man is invincible.

Yogi Bear, it was, as they once knew him, who ran with Greyman to the boozer when their dixie bashing duties were done, to tell the tale of Hatrack and Porky and Pumpkins, retelling it over and over as they drank from the cool cans with feverish excitement, each version slightly more embellished with detail of Hatrack's acute embarrassment, but there were unbelievers.

"No officer and gentleman should ever be caught admitting a mistake nor apologising to his men," Nigel sermonised.

"Then he should be made to," The Chi-Com Man said.

But no one heard him nor knew he was there.

"I think we just had one of our better days," Sniffer was laughing.

"We did," Greyman roared. "We had a win."

"Don't often get one of those," Snowy laughed.

"Strange, isn't it," the eternally sober Nigel pontificated. "How the days when we win somehow seem worse than the days when we lose."

"He must be made to apologise," The Chi-Com Man said again.

This time Nigel heard the anger and determination in that alien voice, and looked toward you coldly. He did not like people who could not face up to the facts.

"And how, exactly, would you go about doing that?"

"I don't know, but fuck it, Nigel, he's a soldier too. Doesn't he have to follow orders like anyone else?"

"He doesn't have to do anything," Nigel said. "As regards us, he can get away with anything he likes."

And of course, that was it. You knew it was the answer the very moment that Nigel said it.

"Then we must make sure he doesn't get away with it," The Chi-Com Man cried.

"There's fuckin' nothing we can do," Nigel insisted.

But The Chi-Com Man knew it wasn't so. There might have been nothing they could do, but The Chi-Com Man wasn't one of them. The Chi-Com Man was a lone wolf, a solitary hunter, who made his own decisions about what could and could not be done.

"So this just gets buried," Sniffer said. "Like everything else."

Like everything else, your brain screamed, like everything else. Like Ap An Quai, like The Pumpkins, and all of his other little acts of bastardry.

"Buried and forgotten," Nigel said sadly.

"It won't be forgotten," The Chi-Com Man swore. "I won't forget."

He wouldn't either. He knew that then. The Chi-Com Man would have his revenge, but the first thing, the most important thing, was that they would have to know who it was. When it was done, they would have to know that it was the work of The Chi-Com Man.

But other people could come up with their own ideas. Greyman, his eyes as foggy as yours felt, leaned across the table. "What we need is volunteers to crap in his bed every night, so that he really fuckin' knows how we feel about him."

"And twice on Sundays," Sniffer roared in approval.

What it lacked in originality, it made up for in enthusiasm.

"What a lot of bullshit!" That was Nigel.

"We should tie him down and forcefeed him twenty-six pumpkins," Daytripper offered, swinging his arms in wild excitement at the thought and bowling over a pile of empty beercans.

"A lot of bloody codswallop," Nigel responded.

"Sign him up as a Buddhist monk," Snowy guffawed. "And let him burn himself in the streets."

"I'll sell him the petrol and matches," Greyman laughed, and fell right off his chair.

"Why not just transfer him to the Yanks," Mickey Wright said ruthlessly. "No-one lasts more than a week with them."

"He'd change that to three days," Sniffer cried.

"You're all up yourselves," Nigel wailed.

On and on they went and through it all, The Chi-Com Man said nothing. The Chi-Com Man was a man of action, not of words. There were no words to be spoken, only deeds to be done. They were all so full of bright ideas and all the while Nigel waved about his dog-bitten paw in protest and telling them that they were all talking nonsense which of course they were. It was just a game to make them all feel better, to let off a bit of steam, destroying the dreaded Hatrack in a ferocious onslaught of imaginings. But in the morning, they would wake up with their hangovers and it would be forgotten, like everything else was always forgotten. Only this time it would not. This time The Chi-Com Man was amongst them, laying in wait for the time when the ranting and raving was done,

108

and they were sleeping, the quiet time, his time.

Yet you could not stay completely silent. Not only was it important that this was done, but also that everyone knew who had done it. The Chi-Com Man.

"I'm gonna go get him now!" The Chi-Com Man roared.

Someone, Nigel probably, had you by the arm.

"Sit down and shut up, you fuckin' dickhead! Haven't you got in enough fuckin' trouble for one day?"

"I don't care. I'm gonna get him. I'm gonna get him."

You were too. You allowed the madness to well up in your body and completely overwhelm you.

"What'll you do, shoot him?"

Anything, anything. Say anything. Shout it, scream it, let yourself go!

"Yeah, that's it. Shoot him, shoot the bastard."

"Don't do that. You'll wake up the cooks."

By this time, they had you down to the floor and you were being sat upon by someone so large that it could only have been Snowy.

"Poor bastard, he's blown his fuckin' mind."

"We gotta get him out of here."

And while such things were being said, you were being utterly crushed to death, but that didn't matter.

"Where's that fuckin' Hatrack. I'll fuckin' get you Hatrack!"

Then they were manhandling you out into the night, Snowy's huge forearms wrapped so firmly about you that it was difficult to breath. There were visions of faces of Nigel, Greyman, Daytripper and each of them seemed to be holding onto some part of your anatomy—they were dragging you to your bed but just for the benefit of the exercise, you put up one hell of a fight. Twisting and squirming, making it hard for them, kicking out savagely, they were big boys and could take it. Forcing an arm free and throw a punch at that face. Take that, you bastard!

"Shit, he hit me!" Sniffer wailed, and fell behind, the victim of a savage haymaker.

Some of the images of that journey are clearer than others. Greyman moving up ahead carrying the case of beer for the after hours party that would be in Nigel's tent, and to which, apparently, you were no longer invited. Nigel to the flank, out of flailing distance, giving orders like a traffic cop.

"Get hold of that arm, Daytripper. Don't let him swing. Lift him, Snowy, keep his feet off the ground."

"You fuckin' try doin' it!" Snowy grunts back in your ear with his hot beery breath.

"Hey you, what's-a-name. Get hold of his legs."

"Mickey Wright, sir."

"Just fuckin' hold him, will ya?"

But mostly it is indistinct shapes struggling in the darkness like a berserk monster of many arms and legs. Whenever Snowy's crushing arms permit you sufficient air, you unleash another outburst in spite of the efforts of Daytripper who, dodging your flailing free fist in deference to Sniffer's misfortune, strives to slap a hand over your mouth.

"Hatrackkkkkkk! I'll fuckin' get you, Hatrackkkkkkkk!"

In your ear, you can hear Snowy constantly grunting with effort—that alone is a considerable achievement, but he manages to maintain his mighty grip until the end of the journey. The others fare less well, as your efforts cast them off on the end of a lashing foot or haymaking fist sending them sprawling and tumbling and cursing into the brambles from where they would immediately spring up and rush back into the fray. Finally, the whole shebang reaches the hoochie you share with Sniffer and Greyman and they force you inside.

Of course, the fight is far from over, but you allow your efforts to lessen now. They thrust you down on the bunk and Snowy sits on you, while the others pant and gasp from the strain of battle.

"Shit, he's gone completely mad," Snowy coughs, you can hear the scratch as he lights that one fag a day that he reckons he actually needs. Wouldn't mind a fag yourself after that effort, but you'll have to settle for Snowy's residual smoke. Take it easy, for a bit now. Out of earshot of CHQ, there's no longer any need to blaspheme the

110

name of Hatrack.

"Do you suppose we should tie him up? " Greyman proposes, when you have always thought him to be a friend.

"Good idea." Nigel grunts. "Get some rope."

The Chi-Com Man thinks it not such a good idea. The only course open now is to play dead.

"Hey. He's stopped," Snowy perceives through his vast buttocks. He removes himself from your decidedly flattened form.

They stand around for a time, pondering this outcome. You have your head turned away, lying still and limp. Nigel, you suppose, is the one checking your pulses.

"Out like a light."

"Pity," Sniffer laments with his bruised jaw. "I was looking forward to improvising a strait-jacket."

"Do we still need to tie him up?" that arch-enemy Greyman asks with altogether too much enthusiasm.

"Nar," Snowy snorts. "The poor bugger's pissed right off the planet. He won't wake up for days."

"Awright, let's go have a beer," Nigel says. "I need one after that."

"Near broke me bloody jaw," Sniffer is mumbling as they stomp outside and head up the way to Nigel's hoochie. To kick on, no doubt about it. You lie there, very still, eyes firmly closed, and listen, to make sure all of them have gone. Only then do you risk a smile.

"Fooled the bastards," The Chi-Com Man says softly.

For a time, you do not move. Discipline and self-control—that's what it's all about. You hear the sounds you are listening for—the faint sound of music, the murmur of voices, the soft pop of the puncturing of beercans and the gulping of their foaming contents. They will be in there with the tent flaps closed, playing poker as always, staying quiet since drinking after boozer hours is definitely not allowed. Ordinarily you would have been right in there with them. A beer would be good right now, after all that struggling. Or a cigarette... But no. The Chi-Com Man does not need these earthly indulgences. The Chi-Com Man is strong and fully self-controlled.

Fairly soon now the generator will shut down for the night and the lights will go out. It is a matter of remaining exactly where you are until then, just in case. Once the area is plunged into darkness, your time will have come; but not before. Nevertheless, it is not easy to lie there like that, perfectly still and eyes closed and with the bumps and bruises of exhausting effort and a gut full of grog: those minutes swell to apparent hours, and sleep knows that it is well overdue. You grit your teeth against the beery fog in your brain, and wriggle your toes to prove to yourself that you are still wake. Several times, you jolt—fearing that you have in fact fallen asleep. As Snowy said, once asleep under these circumstances, there would be no waking for many hours. Too many hours. You would have to hold on. Control, Chi-Com Man, control.

Finally, the light flickers out. The area is plunged into blackness. The Chi-Com Man opens his eyes. It is his time, the time of darkness when he sees most clearly. Wait a moment, let it settle. There are only the sounds you expect to hear—Nigel and his poker game. You sit up in the bunk, and grapple out a fag. The Chi-Com Man will allow weak Griffin this one small risk. You light it carefully in cupped hands to hide the light. All these handy little tactics they have taught you, and now they can be put to good use. You sit there, waiting, waiting. Time is on your side.

It takes about fifteen minutes for the eyes to fully adjust to the complete darkness. There is no moon, but the stars are bright—everyone else will be blinder than you. Sit there dragging with unshaking hands on the cigarette and listening, but there is nothing to be heard that you do not want to hear. You smoke the cigarette right down to the butt—until you can feel it begin to burn your fingers—and then stub it out. Good enough—that is all you need. Just enough time to let them all settle down over there. Now to begin.

You edge your way around to the end of the bunk and fumble about in your gear until you find what you want; a cool, metallic cylindrical object about the size of an aerosol can, but under the circumstances, in fact something far more sinister. Slip it into your pocket. Now go to the tent flap and wait there, have a listen, then crouch down and unlace your boots, pulling them off quietly and placing them beside your bunk. Roll up your trousercuffs a couple of turns—you don't want them flapping when you run, making noise, and now you are ready. Here you go.

Outside, your feet feel the cold hard earth. You follow the path worn along the side of the three four section hoochies, keeping wide of the guy-ropes, until you have reached the line of the front of Nigel's tent. They are getting pretty cheerful and raucous in there, and you spare them a momentary smile. Listen to them, talking in there, keeping their voices down so Bulldog Doyle won't hear them, but The Chi-Com Man hears all. They are talking about someone you used to know.

"Poor old Yogi. Ain't like him, goin' fuckin' mad like that," Sniffer Gibson is saying.

"Remember the nice quiet shy bloke he usta be?" Greyman asks.

"Nobody can remember back that far," Nigel says.

"It's really fuckin' got to him, ain't it," Snowy declares.

"But he just isn't the same bloke he was before he got shot," Greyman persists.

"Who would be?" Snowy wonders.

"I dunno," Sniffer says. "Yogi always took everything far too fuckin' seriously."

"They should never have sent him back," Nigel says cruelly.

Good friends. Good men. But they waste their breath. Griffin is dead. There is only The Chi-Com Man. You sway a little as you stand there, but to be truthful you are almost sober by now—the cold sweat on your face and the adrenalin pumping through your body has seen to that. It's all clear, Chi-Com Man. Move on to the next stage, nice and easy.

You take the path to the toilet block, safest, surest leg of the mission. Innumerable journeys past, nocturnal and otherwise, make it surest—you can move along smoothly with the assurance of its well worn familiarity, and your exposed feet tell you when you are on the cool bare dirt of the path or if you stray to the edge. That horrible low bramble is already regrouping its forces all over the area, and its

113

sharp little spines turn your toes into antennae. It is also safest because, should it happen that you are intercepted on this stage of the journey, you will be able to make easy accounting of yourself. Ahead you can make out the dark shape of the dunny and you go directly to it and stand at the door.

"Hullo? " you call quietly, just to make sure that there is no-one in there. Take your time. Over to the piss-o-phone and take a leak. You need it anyway. Get settled. Look all around. Then go around to the other side of the structure, the CHQ side, and prop against the cold galvanised iron wall. God, it stinks in there—something you aren't inclined to notice when on official business. From this position, you can survey the entire CHQ area; the dark outlines of the rows of four-man hoochies. There is no light to be seen, nor sound to be heard. Final leg. You move around to the other side of the dunny and pick up another path, the one worn in accordance with the bowel movements of CHQ.

There is no margin for error from here on—to be found will arouse instant suspicion, and now you slip along almost on all fours, crouched right down, stopping to listen between each stride. It is slow and awkward and your rumbling belly and fuzzy head are both in firm disagreement with so awkward a posture: still you persist, and finally reach the edge of the rubber plantation, or at least the point where the road up from the airstrip had been cut through. Directly across the road is the company office, and the next hoochie beside it is the one that serves both as Hatrack's office and sleeping quarters. The company office, you know, would be as empty as any self-respecting office at such an hour. You wait again and listen— there is no movement anywhere—not even, disappointingly, the sound of men snoring peacefully in their sleep. In five swift strides, you cross the road and drop down beside the sandbags that surround the company office. Keeping very low now, you move along the edge of the sandbags like a Red Indian, you supposed, or slithering like a snake. You had, as punishment duties in the past, aided in the laying of these sandbag walls and so know this little spot of ground like the back of your hand. Never could you have imagined that

114

such knowledge would actually become useful.

You slip along under the guy ropes to the corner, and go around and most of the way down to the back of the office. Right beside you now, is Hatrack's hoochie, just six feet away. You reach into your pocket and feel the cold reassurance of the canister. All is quiet. You can even, you think, hear the deep, even breathing of Hatrack inside, the breathing of a man sleeping as peacefully as a babe. Sleep on, Hatrack, sleep on. You are sweating heavily, panting a little not so much from effort as from the effects of your earlier debaucheries. You run the cool metal over your sweating brow. It feels good. And then carefully, with your nerves outside your skin and your senses constantly scanning the area like a radar sweep, you inch across those critical six feet. You are now placed just the width of the sandbag wall from Hatrack in his bunk. You have laid a great number of those sandbags too. You can distinctly hear his somnolent breathing now. Very carefully, you hold the canister up in front of your face, wrapping a firm thumb over the lever on its side, and looping a forefinger through the ring, gently easing the split pin free. You take one deep breath—the moment has come, and from now on it will be speed rather than stealth that will count. In a single movement you rip off the lever, and reaching in over the top of the sandbags, lob the canister into the hoochie. There is the sharp twack of the cap coming down, firing the charge, and in the same instant, the thump and rattle of the canister on the duckboards. But even as that happens, you are on your feet and away.

The important thing now is not so much to make your escape without detection—they will all know who it was, but The Chi-Com Man cannot allow himself to be captured in the act. Go quickly, but not so quickly as to allow the chance of mishaps, such as tripping over guyropes, falling down holes, or running into rubber trees. You must retrace your steps exactly, when the temptation is to run like hell: you scamper back around the sandbag wall of the company office on your hands and knees and dash across the road at exactly the same place and at precisely the same angle. This provides your line of march back through the trees. You have covered all that distance before the first cry goes up, presumably from the victim, but once within the cover of the trees, you immediately halt and take to walking instead, and sticking to the path. The darkness is on your side—searching eyes peering out from CHQ might well be able to spot a fast moving object inside the plantation, but never a slow moving one. You walk carefully to the toilet block without succumbing to the desperate urge to look back behind you; only when you are safely behind the galvanised iron wall do you pause to survey your handiwork.

You see little, though there is someone back there moving and calling, and strange things seem to be happening to Hatrack's hoochie. The last likely point of discovery is the possibility that someone might have occupied the toilet in your absence—no-one had. You walk with long, careful strides, down toward Nigel's hoochie, and it is only over the last couple of yards that your will finally cracks and you burst into a sprint and so come charging in through the tentflaps to the great shock and consternation of the men gathered inside.

"I got him! You got him!" you gasp triumphantly.

The members of four section sat about the table, drinking and playing poker by secretive candlelight. With the sudden incursion of this maniac figure into their midst, someone immediately doused the candle in a splash of beer to provide everyone else time to hide their incriminating cans, for in that first instinctive instant, they were sure that it was they who had been got, caught out by Bulldog Doyle on a nocturnal raid. There followed a pause of one full second while everyone sat or stood in the sudden darkness and wondered what to do next.

"I got him! I really did!" you cried again, though only half as excitedly as the initial outburst.

They recovered immediately from their panic, and were more or less able to recognise the invader for who he was.

"Got who?" Nigel's voice came at you from out of the blackness.

"Hatrack! Got him a fuckin' bewdy."

Nigel stood up then, and walked to where he thought you stood, possibly staring at you in complete horror.

"Did you kill him? " he asked and then pushed his way past you to look outside.

"Don't be silly. I got him with a smoke grenade. You should hear him out there, coughing his guts out. Got him a ripper."

Indeed, at that very moment and even at this distance, someone could be heard coughing in terrible distress. Others were now on their feet and also wanting to have a look.

Over there, a dozen strong torches were flashing all about, and you could soon compile the illuminated fragments into a complete picture. Great billows of smoke plumed out from under the flaps of Hatrack's hoochie and rose into the night, if some gigantic spiritual being had taken possession of it. Out in front the figure staggered about, doubling up with each lung-wrenching bout of coughing, while other men, all of them shouting incomprehensibly, were coming to his assistance. Still more men seem to be blindly panicking and going in all directions. Chaos. It was terrific. And then amongst the bewilderment came the strength of order, as the figure of Bull-dog Doyle made himself apparent, if only through his roaring voice.

"What the bloody hell happened?" he demanded of the world in general. "Get a medic, you men."

The voice of Doyle was enough to bring those watchers from four section back to reality. Nigel turned and grabbed you by the shirtfront, giving you a solid jolt. "You dumb fuckin' idiot. He's not going to like this."

"He's not supposed to," you said—quite logically, you thought. You were, to tell the truth, a bit disappointed in Nigel who suddenly seemed bereft of his sense of humour. But Nigel was not a man to dither, and his tactical mind went swiftly into action. "Awright, quickly now. Everyone undress and into bed and look like you've been there all along," and he was already tearing off his own shirt.

"They'll be out in a minute looking for the bloke who did it, and you can bet your balls this will be the first place they'll look. "

But of course, you were not concerned in the slightest about that: "Let 'em come. We've got plenty of smoke grenades. "

"Snowy! Grab him!"

Wham went the mighty bearhug around you from behind.

You would have liked to have told him that all this wasn't neces-sary and that it wasn't you who had done it anyway but the Chi-Com Man, but Nigel was a man in a hurry. "Awright, let's get him to bed. Greyman, you got that rope?"

"Hey, take it easy, you guys," you were gasping with what little air Snowy's python arms allowed you. "I don't care if they..."

"You might not, but we do. Right, get him down."

Down you went and the metal springs screamed their agony, and you could hardly resist the desperation with which your hands were tied to the bedhead and your feet to the end. Amid that flurry of action, just as you attempted further protest, a firm sweaty hand was clamped over your lips. Then Nigel's mouth was inches from your ear. "Now you get this, you fuckwit. You are unconscious. You stay still, you stay limp, no matter what happens. One peep out of you and I'll belt you over the head with a shovel and make it true, got it?"

You shrugged. Since Nigel had decided to take such a strong view of the matter, it was probably wise to play along. But it was disap-pointing—no-one seem to be enjoying the game the way you'd hoped they would.

Bulldog Doyle led the posse over from CHQ and came, as Nigel had predicted, directly to the four section area.

"Right-o Nigel. Get 'em out here."

"On parade, four section," Nigel echoed, in a very sleepy voice.

And they came out wrapped in blankets and towels and, as Nigel put it later, you never saw such a gang of bedraggled, newly wak-ened, bewildered men in all your life.

You lay there listening to a scene so easily imagined, right down to the stern look on Bulldog Doyle's face.

"What's the go, Charlie?" Nigel ask innocently.

Doyle did not trouble himself to answer. You could hear him pace along the line, eyeing each man, and stopped when he came to the place where you weren't standing.

"Private Griffin seems to be missing, Nigel?"

"Oh, shit. I forgot. He's still tied to his bunk."

"You don't expect me to believe that, do you?"

You braced yourself for it. Immediately came the thump of heavy boots on the duckboards behind your back, and the torchlight showed bright red through your closed eyelids. Hold firm, Chi-Com Man, hold firm. This will be the final test of strength.

"He went fuckin' gaa-gaa on us. We brought him back and had to tie him down..."

"How long ago?"

"About an hour."

"Bullshit, Nigel."

There was a pause. And then came a mighty blow to you shoulder—God knows what he hit you with. But The Chi-Com Man is tough and can take it and didn't even flinch.

"See, he's right out of it," Nigel said confidently.

There was another menacing pause. Then you could feel hot breath right on your ear. At that range, Doyle's roar could be fatal, but instead he mercifully offered a grumbling whisper.

"Had a hard night, have you, Yogi Bear?"

The Chi-Com Man was fearless and stayed limp.

"I don't believe you, Griffin. I reckon you've been out and about, having a bit of a wander."

You wouldn't have called it a wander.

But Nigel intervened: "He'd of needed to be Houdini to get out of that lot."

"Houdini, hey? Well maybe he is. I don't know how he did it. All I know is that he did."

"Did what, Charlie?"

"Someone just snuck over to CHQ and chucked a smoke grenade into the boss's hoochie. Bloody near suffocated him. "

When he put it like that, it did sound like something well worth doing. And indeed, a chuckle arose from the others outside. This was the truest test of The Chi-Com Man's willpower, but not the slightest ripple of mirth touched you.

"And you think it was Yogi?" Nigel asked incredulously.

"I know it was," Doyle said coldly.

Another pause. The Chi-Com Man could take it, whatever it was going to be. Suddenly you were airborne as Doyle seized the whole bunk and over-turned it on the floor, sending you sprawling. Things bumped and bruised but you went like a sack of spuds and allowed no reaction. Doyle grabbed you by the hair and bumped your face on the floor a few times, then shook your head, dragging hairs out by the roots, but you stayed limp and even a dribble of saliva ran from your lips, or was it blood. No matter; The Chi-Com Man could last forever. Doyle gave up then, and let you flop back to the floor.

"We've bred you blokes too tough," he said.

He was as right about that as he was about all the rest.

"I don't believe any of this, Nigel," he said finally.

But he had no choice but to lead his posse off in search of other likely suspects.

Nigel and Greyman uprighted your bunk and lifted you back onto it. Still you stayed limp. Had you responded, it would have been with cries of pain. Keep up the game, the strength, let The Chi-Com Man see it through to the end.

"Jesus. Maybe Charlie really hurt him," Greyman fretted.

"Who cares," Nigel replied ruthlessly.

They didn't even bother to untie you, just left you there in your pain and grief to suffer until sleep or was it unconsciousness finally came. And the Chi-Com Man vanished back into the night from whence he came.

10. Rightful Places

The hot morning sun stretched a finger of light under the hoochie flap to strike a point directly between your eyes and pierce fiercely through the skull to broil your brains and incinerate your dreams. You groaned and moved across the bunk, seeking a shadowed spot on the pillow, without daring to open your eyes lest they be burned from your face. Morning, you thought, a new day, and everything peaceful and calm and generally alright. Go back to sleep, and you should have too, had it not been for your foolish mind which then troubled to cast itself backward a number of hours to the last time that you had been awake. It was mostly a blank but what little remained was too unbelievable to abide. You could feel the rope burns on your wrists, and your lips seemed thick and sore and tasted of blood. Shit!

There was no doubt, however much you might have wished to ignore it. Everything was anything but alright! No peace and no calm. You closed your eyes, desperate now in the hope that sleep would restore itself, but it was a hopeless cause. The shock of realisation itself was enough to ensure that sleep would never return. Pretty soon now you were going to have to get up and face up to this, and that was a prospect that could only be regarded as daunting. The only thing to do then was to pull the blanket over your head and pretend to be asleep, and not only for your own benefit either, but that of others. Just try and savour these last few moments of peace before the inevitable disaster struck.

But there was no escape, not under the covers nor anywhere else. Morning had arrived and with it a fate that was utterly unbearable. Bravely you opened your eyes and looked out at the world. Everything was still and quiet—there were no screams of torture to be

121

heard, nor the tramp of the boots of firing squads. In fact, there seemed to be no-one around at all. From where you lay, you could see the bunks of Sniffer and Daytripper, and it was plain that there was no-one under their mosquito nets. But some Good Samaritan had untied the ropes, and arranged you properly under blanket and mosquito net. Under the circumstances, it was helpful to know that someone cared...

Outside, the brilliance of morning began to gush through the tent flap, and your eyes objected to having to process light in such volumes. What you were doing was deciding was whether you were in any condition to move; carefully, you lifted your head, pulled back the thin blanket and diaphanous net, and shifted your feet around and onto the floor. That went alright. Not too bad at all. Maybe you were feeling just fine. Then your head fell on the floor and shattered in a thousand pieces.

"Ohhhhhhhh."

They came and stood about the entrance to your hoochie, peering in at your earthly remains.

"He lives!" Snowy said, far too loudly.

With very nearly sightless eyes, you peered up at them. They came tramping into the hoochie and stood over your ruined, bowed form.

"Ohhhh," you said again.

"He remembers," Sniffer chuckled.

"Ohhhhh, gawd!"

"He does remember," Nigel snorted.

If only to break the monotony, you attempted speech.

"Shit I must have been really pissed."

"Oh, you were, you were," Greyman laughed.

You gazed up as best you could to study their faces, but not one of them seemed to show any expression at all.

"So, what happens now?" you decided to ask. In fact, you had no choice.

"I should imagine," Nigel answered. "That the shit will shortly hit the fan. "

"And me with it," you knew.

"You'd better get your boots on," Nigel said quietly. "I should think there'll be a company parade any minute now."

The surprising thing about that was that it had not happened last night, right then and there. You began making the effort of pulling your boots on, and discovered that you needed to pull off a pair of green army socks first. Socks were something you never wore and certainly not the itchy army issue type. You frowned with the effort of making sense of that as you removed the woolly things, held them up by the toes, and Sniffer claimed them.

"We put 'em on you to cover up your dirty feet," he said. Thought of everything, these blokes.

"I appreciate it," you said, between grunts as you hauled the boots on. "But I'm going to have to own up to this eventually."

"No you won't," Snowy said.

The boots were on but your brainmatter was swirling like a maelstrom and you had to straighten up. Greyman got down on his knees like one of Christ's disciples and began to lace the boots for you.

"You don't need to do that," you lied.

"We haven't got all fuckin' day, you know," Greyman answered.

"Look. I don't want you blokes getting into any more trouble over something I did."

"We already are in trouble," Snowy grinned. "Have been ever since fuckin' Hatrack took over this outfit."

"We've been over to CHQ to recce the damage," Daytripper said, and could not resist a chuckle. "You really did it nicely."

You were puzzled: "Did I?"

Sniffer had to laugh then: "Fuckin' terrific," he chortled.

"Couldn't have done it better myself," Mickey Wright abetted.

You gazed at their reddened grinning faces in amazement. "Is that what you really think? "

"We've done a whip around," Snowy said. "Everyone knows who did it, but they're all pretending they have no idea."

Nigel reached out—you flinched because you were sure he was going to hit you, but instead he tousled your hair. "Yogi Bear. What you did was the best thing done around here in an awful long time."

And they all went quite silly then, thumping you on the back and shaking your hand and slapping you about the shoulders and laughing and all that over-emotional stuff. You weren't really up to all that manhandling yet, and managed to fight them off. "Hang on, hang on. Look, I know you blokes are trying to help but I won't be able to stand by and see other men punished for what I did. I have a fuckin' conscience, you know."

"No-one gives a tuppenny fuck about your conscience," Snowy was saying. "The point is that everyone reckons that what you did was terrific."

"That doesn't change anything."

"Yes it does," Sniffer said. "You just did what we all would have liked to do, if we'd had the guts."

"Yeah," Greyman added. "You said: Hatrack, we ain't gunna take your fuckin' shit no more."

"So it wasn't really you who did it," Sniffer said. "It was the whole fuckin' company."

"And we don't see any reason why you should take all the credit for what we all feel we did," Mickey figured.

You shook your head. But you knew where the final arbitration lay, and looked directly at Nigel. "Do you agree with this?"

"I'm here, aren't I?"

"But do you agree?"

"We are here fighting for democracy, remember? If that's what everyone wants—and it is—then I want it too."

You really wanted a better answer than that, but right then the throaty voice of Bulldog Doyle rose up from CHQ. "Okay, Delta Company, on parade, right now. Let's see yer move, you bastards!"

They had to help you to your feet, and steady you as nausea and dizziness swept over you, but then you were set to go.

"Well," you said. "This is it."

Nigel grinned and landed a soft punch on your jaw. "Yep. Come on, you fuckin' outlaw, let's go."

And you tumbled outside and ran toward the thundering voice of Bulldog Doyle...

...who, it has to be said, was at his bulldog best, in the manner that had not been seen since the days when he made his fearsome reputation on the parade grounds of the training units.

"Come on, you arseholes, get those fucking ranks together, quick smart. Think, laddie, think. Don't tell me you've forgotten how to make three ranks. Right fucking marker. That's the way, boys. Now get ready for it..."

It was awkward in its unfamiliarity but you were ready for it.

"Okaaaaay... Properly at ease... Now... Companeeeeee... Atennnn... SHUN!"

Clump went the boots on the gravel.

"That was fucking awful! Hideous! I've heard you bastards fart in the mornings in better synchronisation than that! Now GET WITH IT! Standaaaaa... TEASE!"

"Steady...."

"Companeeeeeee... Attennnnnnnn... SHUN!"

Crunch!

That time it was perfect, but Bulldog put you through it three more times, just for the sheer bastardisation of it. And every thump of the boots sent shock waves right up through your body to quake in your ruined brain.

But from the corners of your eyes, you could plainly see the scene of the crime, the hoochie opened up to show the musky red splotching of the chemical, and the ground and the trees about it all lightly burnished. And more so Hatrack himself, who stood quietly to the flank as you assembled, his starched greens blotched with the red chemical, his eyes bloodshot, his complexion pale, and in his hand a handkerchief with which he constantly attended his inflamed nose. Perfect, the ghost of The Chi-Com Man whispered on the breeze that rustled the surrounding rubber trees.

Now that he had completed his preliminary torment of the assembled company, CSM Doyle marched over to Hatrack, stamped to attention and snapped a fine salute.

"Your parade, sir."

"Thank you, CSM."

125

It was fortunate that, right at that moment, Hatrack was over-whelmed by a bout of coughing, deep and lung-wrenching, and as a result had to make his address in subdued tones, his voice croaking and constantly breaking, and without any of the fire and ferocity with which these things were normally tempered. The men could see what had been done and what were its effects, and decide for themselves how they felt about it. And perhaps it was that Hatrack conjured so pathetic a figure, that they could see for themselves that some sort of difference had been made, however transient it might have been. That, alone, made it all worthwhile.

He walked on unsteady feet to stand before them, and stood, running his eyes along the ranks. Those eyes stopped when they located yours, but you maintained firm focus on a tree branch in the far distance, directly ahead.

"It has come to my attention that we have a dangerous maniac in our midst—a psychopath with the mind of a child, who has forfeited his right to stand amongst you. This individual has perpetrated a cowardly attack, foolishly irresponsible and infantile. This man, and I use the term loosely, is a danger to us all. Last night he placed my life in jeopardy for had I not awoken immediately, I might well have suffocated. Next time, it might well be yours. I now give that man the opportunity to step forward..."

You hesitated, but really there wasn't any choice. You would have to step forward, to own up. It could not be any other way. But even while you were thinking that, everyone moved. The whole company, in near perfect formation, took one perfect military stride forward. You and a bunch of stragglers were left behind, the stragglers shuffled into line until you were last man to move, when you meant to be first. You stepped forward into your proper place in the line.

Over to the flank, Bulldog Doyle needed to put his hands over his face and turn away.

Hatrack, astonished that his order had been so badly misunderstood, only slowly realised what it meant. He looked for help from Bulldog Doyle but the CSM was teetering on the brink of a complete collapse into helpless mirth. Hatrack looked back, his face dissolving into despair. Grimly he strove to force himself toward a fury, but his health was not up to it, and he could only manage a pathetic sigh. "I see. So it's like that, is it. You fools. This man is a coward. He is probably even stupid enough to be proud of his idiotic prank. But worst of all he is prepared to allow all of you to suffer to hide his own guilt. Because that is the only alternative he leaves me..."

But at that moment, a violent convulsion overtook him and while he coughed heavily into his handkerchief, the men all looked at each other, smiling proudly. You turned to Nigel. "You bastards. You set that up," you whispered.

"Cors we did," Nigel grinned.

"Quiet in the ranks," Bulldog Doyle growled.

Hatrack, was still doubled up by his convulsions, and his handkerchief stained red, perhaps with chemical, or maybe blood. No one cared which.

Finally, he regained control and fought on, his voice even weaker now. "Alright. If that's how you want it... I have no doubt that there are those amongst you who know the identity of this mad animal, but are reluctant to name him out of some false sense of loyalty. Let me tell you that any man may come and see me at any time and name the culprit—your own identity will be kept secret, I assure you."

He wiped his mouth again, and then, after a glance at Doyle who again had to look away, continued. "Until then, I must take the following action. Because of one moron who cannot hold his liquor, all of you will be deprived. The supply of beer is withdrawn herewith and will stay that way until the culprit has confessed, or has been pointed out to me. That is all. CSM, your parade."

Charlie Doyle told you quietly that you were dismissed.

You walked quietly back to the lines and sat on your bunk while the other men set to the task of cleaning and preparing their gear, but you had no enthusiasm for the task.

"Don't talk about it," Nigel said. "Don't do anything about it. Just get through the day and let it all ride until boozer time tonight."

"But the boozer is closed," you murmured.

127

"Just let it ride," Nigel insisted.

Before long, Sergeant Lawson came strutting over to your hoochie, looking unusually sergeant-like with his clipboard under his arm. He stomped formally on the duckboards and consulted his notes.

"Private Griffin."

"Yeah, Henry."

"I was checking my records, Yogi," he said with his slyest grin. "And I noticed that after the last operation, you omitted to hand back one canister, grenade, smoke, red colouration, signalling for the use of. I wonder if I could have it now?"

You felt a shiver of guilt run through your body. One more lie was completely beyond your scope.

"I don't think I have it, sarge," you said.

"Of course you have. You probably just forgot it—left it in your pack or something..."

"I didn't..."

"Let's have a look, shall we?"

He indicated the pack lying muddy and unopened at the end of your bunk. But you couldn't move, so instead Henry laid the clipboard aside and knelt on the floor and opened the pack. From it—impossibly—he withdrew one red smoke grenade. "Ah, here it is," he said, sounding all the more dramatic now that you realised it was all a charade. "Good, Private Griffin. That completes the records..."

He marked it off with a tick, and then stood, slipping the canister into his pocket.

"I'll just backdate that to yesterday afternoon, Private Griffin. Can't have people thinking I'm slack in my job, can we. There."

Still playing it very formal, clipboard back under his armpit, he turned, but hesitated before he went through the flap. "Private Griffin, I knew I could rely on you to see to it that everything is put in its rightful place."

11. The Delta Jack-up

At sundown, the world is at peace, even in a place like Vietnam. It's a sensation that you feel of everything taking a quick breath at the end of the long and tiring day, before rushing on into the activities of night. For the things of nature, there is that pause between the time the day creatures bed down and the night creatures come awake, in the human world it is probably because everyone is indoors having dinner. And the same applied at Nui Dat, where that too was the hour when the men went to mess. The airstrip was devoid of life, no aircraft moving, nor people either. The guns on Nui Dat hill were silent, there was no traffic moving along the distant Route 2 by-pass. In fact, the only thing moving around down there was you, heading on back to the Delta Company area after a day of punishment duties filling jerrycans at the waterpoint. You wandered along the road beside the airstrip, taking your time in spite of the fact that you would miss dinner and have to hassle the cooks to whip up some leftovers. The silence and stillness was everywhere, and you savoured it; enjoying most of all, you supposed, the relief of being away from Delta Company. For away from Delta Company was a good place to be at the time.

The *Delta Jack Up*, as it was called, was now entering its third week. That wasn't what everyone called it. At Task Force they were steadfastly not calling it a *Mutiny*, fearing the complications that entailed—instead it was passed off as 'a transitional period of reorganisation', called TPR, of course. Others, especially Americans and civilians, suggested it was a *Rebellion*, a *Revolution* even, but that was far too grand a term. It was a jack-up, pure and simple. You had checked a dictionary—'collective refusal to comply with authority' it said. That was it, spot-on.

129

What that amounted to was an endless game of cat and mouse being played out between Hatrack and his men which had by now settled down into a routine. Every morning, the men were summoned to the parade and the same questions asked, the same lack of answers given, and the next batch of men, chosen alphabetically, were despatched to Task Force punishment duties. This posed a problem of how to deal with genuine miscreants, who were simply shunted to the head of the list, which must have created an administrative nightmare for someone, keeping track of who was on how many weeks extra duties. Soon, the alphabet was forgotten, and there were more men available for punishment than there were duties for them. Tasks needed to be invented. The RSM got a new brick blockhouse, and all of the Delta Company bunkers were filled in and re-excavated.

You had copped your share—filling jerrycans was one of these—and it was notable that the workload was not evenly distributed over the company. Of course, the whole adventure was common knowledge around Nui Dat, if only because the other units could not have helped but notice that they were no longer being rostered for the punishment duties. They would ask how the jack-up was going and you would say you were jack of it. Most men of other units thought it was a great joke—an opinion that would not have been shared at Delta Company. Task Force too, plainly knew about it, for Hatrack's men had remained virtually non-operational—eight weeks had passed since Ap An Quai, five since the disaster of Operation Tumbarumba, and three since the one-day fiasco of the 'Pumpkins' operation. While they licked their collective wounds, all that inactivity was preying on their minds.

The boozer, naturally, remained closed, for the smoke grenade throwing fiend had yet to confess though he was daily extolled by Hatrack to do so. The men's personal supplies of grog had quickly dried up, but they were not to be defeated that easily. Each night, in twos and threes, they would disappear from the area, and by late evening, Delta Company's hill was virtually deserted. Where they would go was not too difficult to figure out—there were more than a hundred units in the Nui Dat area and each was equipped with an individual boozer, and most of the men in Delta Company had friends in other units.

There were no regulations against men visiting other boozers, but Hatrack felt the matter was covered by the fact that the men of his company were confined to barracks. Bulldog Doyle led a nightly CHQ patrol around the inner perimeter but there were too many ways in and out of the Delta Company area, and under cover of darkness, the men found their training a great asset and could easily evade the patrol. A threat to count heads in the area during boozer hours was to no avail—there were over a hundred men missing the first night, more the second, and Bulldog was not about to go writing out that number of chargesheets.

Mostly, Hatrack relied on the fact that every boozer had only a certain ration of beer available, and that the Delta Company men would put too much pressure on the supplies of the other units, causing a limit to the tolerance of their consistent visits. But the men of Delta Company were careful to remain thin on the ground at most locations, and anyway, were more than welcome in most places because they had become cult heroes of a sort. Hatrack wrote to the other unit commanders asking that Delta Company men be banned from their boozers, but received almost no co-operation, not only because most of the other commanders did not particularly like Hatrack, but more so because, since boozers were off-limits to officers, such an order would have been difficult to enforce. To attempt to police something like that, the various commanders knew, might well result in a similar jack-up in their own areas: something they were not prepared to risk, especially since Hatrack was not faring all that well with his own.

Naturally, Hatrack laid a huge number of charges against individuals, but that too was quickly reduced to a fiasco. The various sections erected scoreboards, and the number of charges against their various members were recorded and boasted about in serious competition.

HATRACK'S CHARGE SHEET SCOREBOARD
FOUR SECTION
Nigel 0
Griffin 11
Mickey 6
Snowy 9
Greyman 4
Daytripper 4
Sniffer 2
Total 39

OTHER SECTIONS
Andy's section 43
Wally's section 41
Nigel's section 39
Lane's section 28
Dooley's section 17
Jimbo's section 13
Lou's section 13
Abel section 12
Parker's Slack Lot 5
GRAND TOTAL 211
KEEP UP THE GOOD WORK, BOYS.

When the boozer was re-opened, there would be a prize of a night's free beer for the section with the most charges against it, and a month's free beer for the individual with the most offences recorded against him. At this point, Andy Kinross's section was holding off the rest and although you and Snowy were vying for the individual honours, four section was running an undistinguished third. This was considered the fault of Nigel, who might have been the only man in the company to retain a clean sheet. Your own impressive tally arose mostly from guilt, primarily insubordination such as protesting that you were given the shitcan run two day's running and one refusing to obey an order not taking part in an inner perimeter patrol. You still felt a bit pissweak about not owning up despite the continued solidarity of the company, and perhaps you were trying to make up for it by keeping yourself on almost constant punishment duties, but really you found all this behaviour just slightly undignified.

While these things had now become a matter of routine and an accepted part of daily life, there were other aspects of the jack-up that were not so. On the second night of the ban, a group of men who remained anonymous staged a raid on the Q-store and made off with the company's reserve supply of beer. Doyle was given the task of making a search for the cache but it was never found. The inner perimeter patrols were extended to cover the CHQ area generally, but were rendered inefficient by a lack of sufficient loyalty to Hatrack by the participants.

On the third night, the next smoke grenade was lobbed into Hatrack's tent, this time yellow, but Bulldog Doyle was on hand to kick it outside.

"Not so funny the second time," Doyle was reported to have commented. Which remark, after he thought about it for a moment, apparently received the sternest of gazes from Hatrack. Three more were thrown, but they were to no effect for Hatrack had now switched quarters and moved in with Doyle. No-one wanted to gas Bulldog, however inadvertently, and Hatrack learned the wisdom of keeping someone popular in his proximity at all times. Like carrying a cobra around your neck to keep the flies away, Bulldog commented.

The raids on the Q-store and kitchen continued unabated, and Hatrack, with the few men he could trust, took to employing his officers and personal staff to maintain the interior patrols. On the first night, the kitchen was raided and when Bulldog Doyle arrived on the scene, he found the patrol, comprising Lt Haig who was commander of Ten Platoon, Quartermaster Tom Modlin and Payclerk Martin, all bound and gagged in one of the cool rooms, and each with the word 'scab' painted on his chest.

"I don't suppose you recognised any of them," Doyle asked as he untied them.

"Not a chance," Haig said. "It was too dark and they were too quick for us. "

Doyle grinned: "These blokes have been chasing the Cong so long they've become like them themselves."

Now Hatrack was forced to embark upon another change of plan. For the interior patrols, he selected from his 'favourites' on the if-you-can't-lick-'em-join-'em basis . The idea was that if offences were committed and the culprits not found, the men on guard duty at the time would face the punishment. That didn't work either, mostly because charges now scored valuable points, or else the raiders merely waited until someone they did not particularly like was on guard before striking. This ludicrous condition still prevailed, with people like Snowy and Greyman volunteering for the interior patrols in their desperation to try and gain the lead. Someone had calculated that it would take two hundred clerks a month to process the paper-work arising from Delta Company charges, and ten officers a year to hear them all.

If Hatrack was having trouble quelling the activities of his men, he fared even worse in his efforts to defend himself. He might, at any time, find something like a dead rat in his pocket, and all manner of foul objects in his bed. Every snake, scorpion and spider found was transferred to his quarters, and there was graffiti slandering him all over the area. Someone, quite disgustingly, actually laid a turd on his pillow. But the coup-de-grace came one day when a gunshot was heard in the vicinity of his tent, and Hatrack rushed into his quarters to find his own Browning pistol lying, still smoking, on the bed. He foolishly picked it up just as Doyle arrived on the scene, along with Holly and Sergeant Lawson as witnesses. Doyle walked up and took the pistol from him.

"Somebody fired that, CSM," Hatrack said.

"So I see," Bulldog said, and looked around. "I don't see anyone."

"CSM, it was not me," Hatrack growled. "Someone crept in here and..."

But Doyle was gazing at the bullethole in the roof of the tent.

"Accidentally discharging a weapon in the base area is a serious offence, sir, irrespective of rank. I'm afraid I must report the matter to the RSM."

"I did not fire that weapon, CSM!"

As a result, the CHQ charge scoresheet gained an extra statistic.

HATRACK 1

It was all a bit childish really, schoolboys defying their strict head-master, and by now you were decidedly weary of it. You found you were ashamed from both points of view—as perpetrator, but also because you were a participant. You wished they would stop, that the company would become operational again, and you could get back to whatever passed for normality. You felt uncomfortable, caught up in something that there was no way out of, and thus obliged to play along, fulfilling your role as unit martyr. You had other misgiv-ings, especially because you had retained your close relationship with Nigel, and talking to Nigel about such things did little to raise your enthusiasm.

Nigel was a man left out in the cold. No-one talked to him much, and he didn't particularly want to talk to them either. His eyes had grown cold, his expression dark. The spring had gone from his stride, and his moustache no longer bristled with excitement. He was, you could tell, extremely disappointed in you, and that hurt deeply. You owed, you were sure, a great deal to that man, and he was your friend as well as your leader. Now, it seemed, he regarded you as a betrayer.

"They should never have sent you back, Griffin," he said to your face, in just the way you knew he said it to others. And if you might have perfectly agreed with that sentiment, you still did not much like the reasons behind his saying it.

You would visit him in his hoochie where he sat alone, sipping from his battered tea mug, rubbing his troubled brow.

"All this anti-Hatrack bullshit," he said grimly. "They just don't have a leg to stand on."

You had to admit that you were surprised at first that even Nigel could reach that sort of conclusion.

"What about that bullshit with the pumpkins?"

Nigel shrugged: "Hatrack had to take the action that he did be-

135

cause he was worried about the morale of his men. He knew if he let them get away with that, others would try similar things. It's hard, you know, but true enough. What we're seeing right now shows pretty plainly that these blokes' capacity to stay in line is very fragile. He knew, all along, that he had a rebellious mob of reluctant conscripts on his hands, and that he would have to take the tough line to keep them under control. We thwarted that. Like we thwarted everything else he tried."

"And what about Ap An Quai?" you asked. It was the burning question.

"Yes," Nigel said sadly. "Ap An Quai lies right at the bottom of all this. This rebellion is in fact a direct reaction to that battle. But what did Hatrack do wrong? He had orders to hit the place before nightfall, and he had to follow them."

"If possible," you said.

"Yep. And it was possible. We took the fucking place, didn't we? Sure, we got knocked around a bit, but how much do you blame that on Hatrack and how much on the conditions at the time? The truth is, we went in there slack and got barrelled. Hatrack's plan was good because it worked, even in the adverse circumstances. And the task was feasible because the job got done. This is a bloody war, Yogi, not a Sunday school picnic. People are supposed to get hurt from time to time, and other people are supposed to learn to live with it."

You felt a bit ashamed at hearing all this. "So it isn't really Hatrack that's to blame. It's the whole fucking war, the fucking system."

Nigel could smile. He looked at you as if you were a young, wide-eyed boy, anxious to gather in whatever enlightenments a father could pass on.

"The real trouble, Yogi, is conscripts. Conscription does not work. It makes for slack and fairly useless armies. You weaken an army by drafting people. Without the draft, your army would be much smaller, but they would all be professionals and they'd do far better. "

He regarded your expression of dismay and offered a sympathetic smile. "Now, I'm not saying that conscripts themselves aren't any good. You're tough enough, got the guts and got the ability. Ap An Quai proved that. But you conscripts think too much about what you're doing—you're still civilians at heart. It doesn't matter to you blokes that you won the Ap An Quai battle, that it was in fact a major victory. All you can think about is that we got plastered, and you've never got over it. And I don't think you ever will."

Words of that sort can ring in your brain on still evenings. Walking along the elevated embankment of the road beside the airstrip, you neared the Delta Company area with a sense of dread. You did not want to be there, to be a part of all that, and you were dawdling, suspending as long as possible your arrival. Up there, the madness would still be going on, and you did not want to be a part of that madness, did not want it to be a part of you. It had become like a disease, a disease that ate its way into every corner, every part, of the body. The very inescapability of it all, and the futility. You knew there was only one thing in the world that you wanted, and that was to go home. You still had three months to go before your time would be up. It was bad enough to know, as you had always known, that you would remain a prisoner for those three months yet. It was worse to be sure, to know only too well, that the coming three months were going to be the very worst of your life, far worse even than the nine months that had gone before. You were a dead man, still walking, awaiting his rebirth, but that rebirth, you could see, remained forever away. It was just like Skull Braddock said: no matter how bad things had got since the day you had entered the army, they steadily got worse. It had become a pattern now, far too clear to be denied. It was hard to imagine things being worse than this, but no longer was it hard to conceive the idea that the unimaginable worse condition would very soon exist. You could be pretty daunted by thoughts like that.

And already, it seemed, the movement toward that disaster was underway, if the things you heard were true. Some of the men you had been working with that afternoon at the water point had been from BHQ, and they had a story to tell. The word was that Porky had offered Hatrack an ultimatum and done so in the strongest possible terms. "I don't care how, Major," the Battalion Commander was reported to have said. "but I want Delta Company returned to an operational condition immediately. The other companies are complaining about their extra work in the field and rightly so."

"The punishment doesn't work, sir," Hatrack protested. "They just make a mockery of it."

"You must dispose of the sources of the trouble, Major. Pick the ringleaders—I don't care who or why—and throw them out of the company. You name them, I'll remove them—no questions asked."

"Yes sir."

"But major, make damned sure they are the right ones. Because after them, the next man to go will be you."

What it amounted to, then, if the story was true, was a purge, and it would not have been good, the relaters of the story thought, to have been in Hatrack's boots right then. You could not help thinking that there might have been a number of pairs of boots that it might not have been good to be in around Delta Company at the moment, and you suspected that one pair of those may well have been the very ones you were wearing now.

You reached the Delta Company perimeter just on nightfall, and indeed, the signs were plain enough. The first thing you noticed was that there was no one at the gate to check you in, a practice that had been adopted since the beginning of the jack-up. In fact, there wasn't much sign of anyone. You walked in along the road through CHQ, looking about, quite puzzled. No sign of the guards on the Q store, nor the kitchen. No trace of the interior patrol. And then, it occurred to you that something else was different. There was a sound that was distant, both physically and in terms of memory, but very familiar. Voices, many voices, jovial and raucous, over there, that way, in the direction of the boozer. You turned that way to investigate, but then remembered that you were still carrying your rifle, and rifles were never at any time allowed in the boozer. You would drop it off in your hoochie... but it did seem that the Delta Company boozer was finally open again.

Arriving at the four section lines, you could see that Nigel was still about. Stepping into his hoochie, you pulled up short. The place was in a terrible state of disarray, and in the midst of it all stood Nigel in the process of packing his belongings into his trunk.

"What's going on, Nigel?"

"I'm going places," he muttered, mostly into the interior of his trunk where he was carefully laying his neatly folded greens.

"Where?" Though it had already occurred to you what the answer was.

Nigel stopped what he was doing and turned to look at you. You had the distinct impression that you were interrupting something, and that you were the last person that he might have wanted to be standing there. He stood up, arching his back to ease the stiffness and answered whilst still locked in that posture. "Out of this fucking company, that's where."

"Out.... ? "

You were frowning, far from willing to believe what was only too plain: "Are you serious?" you asked, when it was ridiculously obvious that he was.

Nigel looked at you—his great moustache seemed to be askew, certainly his face looked crumpled. He sighed, and plainly decided that people who asked such moronic questions did not deserve an answer.

"Why don't you go over to the boozer and have a beer, Yogi. It's open again, you know."

"I noticed," you said. But couldn't for the life of you think of anything else to say.

Right at that moment, two figures came in the rear entrance of the hoochie. Snowy and Greyman, and both looked pretty grimfaced as they stomped in and sat themselves on Nigel's bunk, a matching pair of toy soldiers who looked like they had just been outgrown.

"Thought you might want a hand, Nigel," Snowy said flatly.

"Don't," was all Nigel answered.

But they sat there, and seemed to be suffering that same helpless paralysis that you were. You felt cold, and quite ill. Things were, you knew, badly wrong, and the sorrowful expressions of Snowy and

Greyman only served to confirm that.

"What the bloody hell is going on?" you demanded.

Nigel looked as though he was about to jump up and hit you then, but instead he went on with his packing, and refused either to speak or hear you.

"Nigel's been sacked, Yogi," Snowy said solemnly.

"Sacked? But why?"

"For being in charge of the wrong fuckin' section, that's why," Nigel erupted, his hostility intensifying rapidly.

"Nigel has been blamed for the jack-up," Greyman said, and sounded no less exasperated with your stupidity than Nigel. "Hatrack's ripped his stripes off him and chucked him out of the company."

Anyone you like, Porky had said, no justification needed. But this was nonsensical.

"But how can he do that?"

Nigel slammed down the lid of his trunk and glared at you in extreme irritation. "Because fuckin' Hatrack, contrary to current beliefs, happens to be in charge around here and like I told you blokes, time and again, he can do any fuckin' thing he likes."

Shrivelling under that heated blast, you reeled over to flop into Nigel's deckchair, largely because your knees seemed to be sagging under the weight of comprehension.

"But that's fuckin' stupid. Shit, Nigel. You're the last person he could rightfully blame."

You were probably, you realised, the hundredth person to make that statement in the last few hours, but what else could you say.

"Try telling that to Hatrack," Nigel said.

There was suddenly no longer anger, but resignation in Nigel's voice, a muffling of his tone that said it was all too late. Gracious defeat rather than hopeless conflict. But you were far too agitated, shocked, incensed, to accept that.

You sprang to your feet: "I will too!"

"Don't you think you blokes have caused enough fuckin' trouble, Yogi!" Nigel bellowed at you.

And because he could see that he had knocked a pretty sizeable dent in you, Nigel calmed, softened, became sympathetic. While the best you could do was try to convince yourself that this was all some sort of monstrous joke .

"Awright, listen," Nigel was saying. "He said that I was the instigator of all the trouble—that ringleader I was telling you about. He said I was a troublemaker not fit to run a section and that he had to make an example of me. And he whipped off my stripes and threw me out of the company, effective immediately."

Your stomach felt as if it was being twisted on a skewer. "I seem to have heard it all before," you said. "But damn it, Nigel, he's dead fuckin' wrong."

Even you could see you were making a scene about an issue that was resolved, no matter how unsatisfactorily. Nigel had just about finished his packing, and that would be that. Hatrack was an officer in the army and under no obligation whatsoever to be right or fair.

"He's not, you know," Nigel was saying to the contrary. "Hatrack's assessment of the situation was that the trouble generated out of this section, and as the leader of the section, I was responsible. All of which is quite true."

"It doesn't matter. Someone should go to him—tell him that you didn't play any part in what happened..."

But Nigel shook his head. "Not the point, I'm afraid. The fact is that it was not enough for me to ignore the situation. As section leader, it was my job to keep you blokes in line—that's what they were paying me for. I stopped doing it, and they've stopped paying me. Simple as that."

Simple as that. You shook your head, but the disbelief was fading now.

"Are you the only bloke he sacked? "

"At the moment," Nigel said. "He re-opened the boozer and said that if there is any more trouble, more blokes would go. And he'd keep chucking them out until there was no-one left if necessary. But I don't think there'll be any more trouble."

And all too soon, he was packed and ready and the vehicle came up to transport him and his gear down to BHQ. He shook no hands, nor did he make any other sort of parting gesture. You helped him load his gear taciturnly, and the other members of the section appeared and gathered about. And then, he climbed in the vehicle carrying precariously his mug of tea that he had just now brewed. Finally he looked up and said in a bitter tone. "Well, you're in charge now, Yogi Bear. You can take responsibility for these dickheads. Me? I'm glad to be out of it."

You had to look away. You could find no answer to make either. Nigel chuckled then, and for a fleeting instant, his old self reappeared. "Well, I hope you guys appreciate me getting the boozer opened for you. Have a nice war," and then to the driver: "Awright, let's go."

And he raised his mug to you, and was whisked away. You stood watching the vehicle pass from your view in a cloud of dust.

"Well, that went well, didn't it," Snowy said.

"That isn't even nearly funny," you bit at him.

"Nar," he said. "Same old jokes but they just aren't funny any more."

Within an hour of Hatrack's decision, Storeman's Clerk Private Robert 'Nigel' Naughton reported for duty at the Battalion Quartermaster's office.

12. Charlie on the Line

There is this ringing sound which, fair fuckin' dinkum, sounds for all the world like a fuckin' telephone. All over, Red Rover, your poor fuckin' brain's completely rooted. Sniffer, forward scout, is fifteen yards up the track, and he stops and turns to offer you a baffled frown. It is a relief to see that he has heard it too. He holds his fist to his cheek, just like someone talking on the phone. You nod. Then you point at several imaginary spots on the track in front of you—find it. You look back toward Daytripper, touch your hand on top of your head and he keeps coming forward, in long careful slow strides, lugging Mabel, until he reaches your side.

"Do you hear that ringing?" you ask in a whisper.

"Of course I hear the fuckin' ringing," Daytripper grunts, a little louder than you would have liked.

"Sounds like a telephone," you say, to make a complete dickhead of yourself.

"Telefuckingphone," Daytripper snorts in disgust.

You wave him through, to back up Sniffer.

Absurd? You bet, but you were willing to believe anything these days. You were, after all, in the remotest part of the jungle in the remotest part of the province, following a small narrow track that showed no sign of being used for a very long time. Hatrack had halted the company when the track was discovered, and while the rest of them had a nice rest and some lunch, you were instructed to take four section five hundred metres down the track and see what you could find. It is just about the turn around point now, when you checked with Mickey Wright a few moments ago, it was four twenty. But now there is this ringing that has to be investigated.

You squat at the side of the track while Sniffer goes forward, very slowly and very carefully, sticking right at the edge of the track, and Daytripper with him, Sniffer head down, Daytripper head up. That's the way boys. The rest of the patrol moves through. Snowy is carrying the radio, a luxury for such a small patrol. When he is with you, you whisper. "Tell them we're checking out a strange ringing sound."

Snowy speaks softly into the handset, and then looks at you, grinning.

"He said to get your ears flushed out."

You just nod. What more could you expect? You keep Snowy at your side and wave Mickey through.

"How many paces, Mickey?"

"Four six three."

"Help Sniffer find that fuckin' thing."

"Sounds like a telephone."

"I know. But you can bet it wasn't installed by the PMG."

The last man is Greyman. You wave to him to stay where he is, a turn around signal to tell him to watch your backs. All set. Now to find that bloody telephone.

It stops ringing, but by then, Sniffer is waving excitedly and pointing his rifle into the scrub nearby. You go forward, Snowy at you heels with the radio like a faithful hound. You look where Sniffer is pointing and, finally, see the thin black wire stretching low down through the scrub. You follow the line, and there it is.

It is an old field telephone with Chinese markings, wedged down between a couple of giant exposed roots. It looks like it has been there for quite some time, but there are greasy marks in the centre of the handpiece. Someone has used it very recently. It is probably a listening post for a larger Charlie camp on the other end of that cable. And since it has been ringing, it poses in your mind probably the very same question that is in the mind of the Charlie soldier on the other end of the line: what the fuck has happened to the bloke who is supposed to be here answering the call? You look around very edgily, and sneak along in the scrub a few metres following the telephone wire. Yes, someone has passed along here before you, there are broken stems, very fresh. Someone in a hurry. The scenario constructs itself in your mind. The sentry has been sitting here when he hears you coming, has lacked the nerve to stick around, pick up the phone and tell the base, and has instead run off to deliver the warning in person. You look over at Daytripper, and give him a thumbs down signal, then toward Sniffer. That will keep them alert. Because by now, you can be reasonably certain, the Charlies in that camp will know exactly where you are. Crouched down then with Snowy behind the tree, you take the handset of the radio and speak into it, keeping your voice low.

"Four Two Bravo for zero-alpha."

"Zero-alpha," crackles the reply in your ear. Mumbles Dorset.

"Four Two Bravo. Fetch Sunray. Over. "

Zero-alpha Sunray is the general code for whoever is in charge, which in this case meant Hatrack. His voice crackles on the line.

"Zero-alpha for Four Two Bravo, Sunray speaking over."

"Four Two Bravo. We have located a telephone of...."

"A what?"

"Four Two Bravo. A telephone, people, ringing up, for the use of. Definitely Victor Charlie. Operators are definitely in the vicinity, over."

There is a pause on the other end while Hatrack thinks that through.

"Zero-alpha. Your call sign is now Four Two. What is the relationship of the track to the telephone cable, over?"

"Four Two. Not really parallel but in the same general direction, over."

"Zero-alpha. Right, Four Two. Leave a man to indicate position of telephone, and then continue your patrol for another five hundred metres. We will be backing up behind you, over."

"Four Two. Roger wilco, out."

"Zero alpha. Be careful, Four Two. Out."

"Four Two. Affirmative. Out."

That 'be careful' is not really an expression of concern for your personal safety, but an indication to you that Hatrack knows only too well the possible danger he is placing you and the others of four section in. What it means is that you could have disputed the in-struction—that you do not have to follow the orders any more than you want to. His plan is quite plain. He will bring up the rest of the company and see where the telephone cable goes to. In the mean-while, you will be placed five hundred metres ahead of the company. The cable is not likely to be any longer than that, and when the Charlies abandon their position, as they surely will when the com-pany swoops down upon them, there is every chance that they will use a track to do so, perhaps this track, and four section might be able to catch them in an ambush. If it does place four section in considerable danger, it is, on the other hand, not an unreasonable plan.

And that call-sign change? Four Two Bravo is a section patrol, Four Two is platoon sized. Just in case the nasties are tuned in, he's trying to kid them that there's more of you than there really are.

You look around at the others and quickly outline the scheme.

"Greyman, you count the paces. Mickey, you stay here and show them where the telephone is. Keep out of sight. Let's get going."

You could see them looking a little bit nervous and you couldn't blame them for that. But the danger is not as great as might be imagined, at least not if things go true to form. If your original scenario is correct the Charlies at the other end of that telephone would already know that the Uc Dai Loi are about to descend upon them, and have abandoned their position and be long gone before you get close enough to be in any danger. On the other hand, if they did not know the Uc Dai Loi are coming—the sentry having been struck by lightning or perhaps a deserter—then it would be the com-pany following the telephone line, rather than four section, who would contact them. All quite reasonable, except that to rely on such suppositions, no matter how likely they seem, is a sure way to get into trouble.

"Hatrack says be careful."

"I'll bet he did," Greyman says. "The bastard's still trying to get us wiped out."

You grin, and signal Sniffer to lead off.

"Take it away, Sniffer. Straight down the track, nice and easy."

This was the Chinese New Year—Tet, as they call it—and with it the long outstanding promises of Chairman Ho regarding the destruction that they would wreak upon their enemies were put into effect. Nearly every·major town and base in South Vietnam was attacked in the space of a couple of days—for Charlie it was a staggering effort, an aspiration far beyond their capabilities, and yet so outrageously ambitious, this mighty unified attempt to seize control of the country and drive the American Imperialists and all their running dogs into the sea. A do or die effort. They died mostly.

From all over the country came reports of massive battles. The Americans were content to sit within their defences, using their enormous firepower to mow down wave attacks, while the South Vietnamese Army was employed as a strike force to try and break up the invading Communist forces pouring down from the north. The Americans established a giant base right on the powerline that led from the Ho Chi Minh Trail into Saigon; it would be necessary for the invading force to capture that base before they could proceed, and the Americans were defending it grimly. But that sort of fighting was not what the Australians were good at, and they dealt with the situation the way they knew best—the only way they knew.

In platoon and company sized patrols, they combed the area about the base, continually striking the leading edge of the Communist forces whenever and wherever they might. These contacts came thick and fast—Delta Company alone was averaging three daily. In daylight, they were the fast, frantic, hit-and-run contacts, by night it was Charlie running into Australian ambushes. All over the country, an incredible carnage was taking place and the dead being counted by thousands daily, but the Australian casualties were minimal. Another cat and mouse game—you were getting to be pretty good at this.

Sniffer creeps along the track at the slowest of slow rates, and you are happy to follow suite. A pause after each carefully placed step, looking about all the time, listening intently, then the next careful step. Five hundred metres can be a long distance at this speed, but you are in no hurry. You do not want to get any further away from the rest of the company than you have to. The order of march is altered now, with Snowy sticking right beside you with the faintly hissing radio headset pressed against his ear.

"They've linked up with Mickey," he whispers.

You nod. You wish Mickey was here. Your patrol is only five men— he would add better balance. But someone had to stay to direct them to the telephone. Five men, out on a limb, while behind them someone might be sawing it off.

It is for Sniffer to spot any trouble up ahead. You are busy enough keeping your eye on him, watching the compass to try and keep track of the bearing, spasmodically tuning in to Snowy. Behind you, Daytripper has the job of keeping the patrol in formation, for with Mabel, he possesses three-quarters of the section firepower, and so has to keep every man within his range of vision at all times in case they might suddenly need his covering fire. Not far behind him is Greyman, counting the paces and practically walking backwards as he covers your rear.

Sniffer, edging along, stops every couple of steps and looks back at you. There would be a log that might be hiding something, a bend in the track, anything at all. Although on every occasion you signal him to continue, he never fails to check each time he encounters a variable, and neither should he. Finally you raise your hand, signalling a stop. You reckon it is five hundred paces, and look back at Greyman. He holds up five fingers.

They do not need to be told to deploy. Daytripper and Greyman go off the track a couple of paces to cover the area ahead of you, Sniffer backs up to join you and Snowy, retiring into the bush between you, and an ambush is automatically laid. Snowy, without any instruction from you, speaks into the handset: "Four Two for zero-alpha. Task accomplished, over."

The radio is tuned to so low a volume that from only two yards away, you hear nothing except an interruption in its normal faint hissing as the reply comes through.

"We're to wait," Snowy says.

148

You are gasping for a cigarette, but it is too risky. You looked one way toward Sniffer and Snowy, then the other toward Daytripper and Greyman. They sit silently, watching and listening, their faces lined with strain, as no doubt your own is. You will wait. You do not allow yourself to think beyond that point.

Then Snowy is grinning broadly and looks at you. "The phone's ringing again," he reports, and hugs the handset closer to his ear to get a better picture of what is going on. You already have your picture—blank-faced men standing there and looking down at the jangling instrument.

"What do we do?" they would ask each other.

"Answer it," Hatrack, that master tactician, would say.

"Ky is answering it," Snowy reports to you. Ky is the company's Vietnamese interpreter, a bouncy jovial little man who speaks a perfectly eloquent pidgin English.

"It is the Viet Cong, sir," Ky reports.

"Ask him where he is?" Hatrack orders brilliantly.

"He says, you must come try to find him."

"You tell him," Hatrack says hotly. "Many Uc Dai Loi will come and shoot the shit out of him."

Ky smiles: "He say, many Viet Cong there. They shoot shit at us too. They not afraid."

You smile. It is a challenge that cannot be ignored. But really there is nothing to smile about. What it means is that the Charlies are still in their camp, and now they will leave. And that is where you and your undermanned ambush will come in.

Snowy hands the handset to you: "Hatrack wants to talk to you."

The hissing black instrument on the end of its spiral cord might well be a viper, such do you handle it.

"Callsign is Four Two, not Four Two Bravo," Snowy reminds you. You nod, and speak softly into the mouthpiece. "Four Two for zero-alpha. Sunray speaking. Over."

"Zero-alpha. What bearing are you on? Over?"

"Four Two. Two seven four, over."

"Zero-alpha. Accurate? Over."

"Four Two. Inaccurate. The track winds a lot. But close. Over."

"Zero-alpha. Roger, Four Two. Go another five hundred metres. As long as the bearing does not decrease. Over."

"Four Two. Roger. Out."

"Zero-alpha. And be double careful, Four Two. They might have you tagged. Out."

"Four Two. Roger. Out."

You pass the handset back to Snowy. Yes, Hatrack, double careful. This is getting pretty dicey now. They might have you tagged, Hatrack says. What he means is that if a smart Charlie who could speak English has his radio set tuned in on your frequency he would be able to figure out exactly where you are, for he'd know the original position of the telephone, and that you have proceeded five hundred metres on a bearing of 274 degrees and are now about to go five hundred more on the same bearing. You continue to pretend to be thirty, rather than five men, but that is the name of the game—confusion of the enemy—but if the telephone operator is no mere braggart and there are many Viet Congs to shoot shit at you, they are all going to be in an awful lot of trouble.

There are a few other things that bother you. Hatrack and the company now would set off following the telephone wire, which appears to run on a bearing of about 270 degrees, which means that you are now placed wide of the camp by four degrees over a thousand metres, in other words, probably less than fifty metres to the flank of the camp, probably a lot less. And the Cong are still there, preparing either to bug out or else stay and fight. Which means that you would have to be pretty bloody close to them. Desperately trying to keep your voice calm, you point these little matters out to the others before you move off. There are no smart answers to report: they take it in silently.

Sniffer goes along even slower, and checks back to you more often. But the tension is on at the rear of the line as well, where Greyman, walking backwards, knows only too well that if the Charlies are a bit slow leaving the camp, they might well come hurtling along the track straight up your bum. Thus you creep along, mere faint shadows in

150

the patchwork shade of the jungle, barely there at all. After two hundred and fifty paces, you raise your hand to Sniffer to stop and summon Snowy and his radio over.

"Four Two for zero alpha. Bearing is now two seven two. Over."

"Zero-alpha. Wait. Over."

It is bringing you in too close. Too close to everything.

"Zero-alpha for Four Two. Roger your message. Proceed. Over."

"Four Two, roger wilco. Out."

"Zero-alpha out."

It is no longer Hatrack but Mumbles Dorset to whom you speak. Proceed, Hatrack has told him to say. You wave Sniffer on again. What you are noticing now is that your sixth sense is not operating, which you would have understood to mean that there weren't any Charlies anywhere around here. You are feeling very tense, and so you ought to be, but that strange calmness that usually indicates impeding trouble is not present at all. Yet you are sure, have been assured, that there are Charlies about. But that was the fuckin' trouble—it only worked sometimes. In any case, you weren't about to rely on such nonsense. Still you are sure. There are no Charlies around here. And in being sure, it convinces you of something else. That something is going badly wrong.

Then Sniffer stops, and looks back and his expression says that he has the same feeling. He raises his hand slightly, and you pass the gesture back on down to the others. You stand there on the track, stockstill, immersed in listening. The faint rustling comes to you, barely perceptible, but it is all you need. Movement, over there in what would have been the most logical direction for the camp. You turn swiftly and give the signal to deploy into ambush. Quickly, yet without haste, you drop off the edge of the track to the left, placing it between you and the movement. And there you lay prone, weapons cocked and thrust forward, five metres apart, and strive to get your thumping heartbeat under control in order that you could better see and hear and know what it is out there. Getting the breathing right, getting the firing position comfortable. Snowy murmurs into the handset. "Four Two for Zero Alpha. We have movement. Out."

Daytripper snaps up the sights on Mabel and nestles the butt into his shoulder, while Greyman arranges the spare belts of ammunition. You check the AK over, and slip the safety catch. And you wait. Oh, they're there, alright. Not the slightest doubt about that. The rustle of men moving through that dense jungle is all too plain. A lot of men too, and not going to a great deal of trouble to be quiet about it. You can distinctly hear the twigs snapping under their boots, the brushing of the leaves and branches on their clothes, the occasional clunk of a metal weapon striking a treetrunk, the thump of a boot on a root. The question is, where are they, or at least, how far away and which direction they are going. Visibility is at best twenty-five metres—less from your prone position beside the track. You have to lie there listening, trying to figure direction, distance, number, collecting all the sounds you hear into a single picture. It seems that they are off the track and not coming directly toward you, but will pass you by at a point about fifty metres into the scrub. Perhaps...

You look at Snowy who is next to you, and indicate with your hand a line running parallel to the track. He nods. You show him five fingers with your hand reversed. He nods again. Your assessment, you can only assume, is correct. They will pass fifty metres from you. The next question to be answered is whether you want them to pass by or not. It is a matter of how many of them there are, and what sort of people. To hit a force from ambush is not necessarily an advantage. You can all too easily picture a force of two hundred well-armed North Vietnamese regulars who know they are being pursued by fifty Australians, and, when ambushed, know the ambushers number only five or six men. They would go straight through you—it would be suicide. On the other hand, if you were to hit them, it should be done before they begin to pass you, thus driving them back onto the company which, you have to assume, is coming up hard behind them but still about five hundred metres away. On the other hand, they might not know anything about you. They might only be women and children evacuating while the men stay behind to meet Hatrack's threat. The possibilities are endless, and you figure you have about one minute left in which to make your decision.

You need to know more, and there is only one way to do that. The risk has to be taken. You look at Snowy and your fingers do a mime of going for a walk, then play a little boys game of looking through imaginary binoculars. Snowy nods. Daytripper raises his arm to indicate the extent of his arc of fire—you will have to keep yourself beyond that line if you want to stay out of the crossfire. You slip off your pack and web belt, load three pockets with magazines, and offering the others a rather helpless shrug to which they either wink or smile, you set off.

Over the track first, the most exposed part, easing along on your belly like an alligator. And then into the jungle on the other side. Wait and listen. They are still coming on, but still a safe sort of distance, as much as any such short distance can be safe. Slowly, you raise yourself onto your knees and look about. That twenty-five yard maximum visibility opens up to you now, but that is all. They are still further away than that. You can go, the sounds of their movement tells you, another twenty metres away from the track—half the distance between their apparent line of march and the ambush. That should take you close enough to see something. You will have to make your decision then—if you are going to attack, you will simply start shooting yourself and Daytripper and the others will follow suit. If you are not, you will probably have to lay low until they pass, for there will be little chance then of sneaking back to the others without being detected. For that reason, you pick a good hiding place over there, and begin to creep toward it, crouched very low. It is that old one step at a time trick. You look at the ground and spot a place where your boot can be placed without making any sound, put your boot there, then look toward the approaching men, see nothing, look for where to place your next step. You get about halfway to your hiding place, and that is all.

All you see is a fleeting shadow, momentarily glimpsed, and nothing more. But that is all you need. You are caught in the middle, and duck down, but it is already too late. As the figure pumps off his first instinctive shots, you dive forward, throwing yourself prone and swing the AK around into the firing position. You can no longer see anything and aren't looking anyway—you simply expend a complete magazine in the direction of the shadow. The AK pummels your shoulder as the bullets rip away on their brilliant streaks of tracers, and at the same time, other tracers flash over your head. There is an absolute deluge of gunfire for about a second and a half, from other men with the shadow, and from Daytripper and the others to the flank. The trees and bushes about you are splintered, their fragments flying everywhere and more dirt and shit fly up in front of you from bullets falling short. But really you are aware of none of it. You are ripping off the empty magazine and about to reach into your pocket when, in spite of the deep thumps of shots and the fierce whiplash crack of them streaking over your head, all those individual sounds so numerous that they are in fact one single deafening one, still you hear something else quite distinctly. A human voice that should have been utterly drowned out, and yet somehow pierces its way through to your senses.

"Holy shit, fucking Jesus," someone over there yells.

Your reaction is instantaneous—there is no time to be horrified yet. You roll your head toward Daytripper and the others and bellow at the top of your voice. "Hold your fire! Hold your fucking fire!"

No more than five seconds will have elapsed by now since those first shots, but in those five seconds, probably two hundred rounds have been expended in that small area. And then, through the duration of the next second, stops. Though it is only partly due to your command. Snowy has been saying on the radio. "Four Two in contact."

But then he heard Dorset saying. "Zero Alpha in contact."

Snowy immediately pounced on Daytripper and stopped him, for Daytripper, blazing away with Mabel could never have heard any mere human voice. Then other men, everywhere are calling ceasefire, and it stops. You all lay there, the echoes of the gunfire stalking away from you, far out into the jungle. And then silence. From ahead of you, a single, unrecognisable voice rises up. "Is that you, Yogi?"

"My fuckin' oath it is."

"Ohhhh, fucking hell!"

154

You drop the AK and close your hands over your face. Oh fucking hell is right. And then, with some desperation, you jump up, quite unarmed and start forward. You only make about three strides before you see it. A thin, dark line, etched along the jungle floor—the telephone cable. You can only stand there staring at it in dismay. One more second and you would have seen it, and this would have been averted. But that extra second has been denied you, and that is all.

Standing there, small tremors of disbelief running through your body, when the truth is all too plain. It is carried by the voices calling with hysterical urgency for medics, by the curses of anger and anguish of other men, and by one voice that screamed intolerably. That screaming man, the single piercing monotone broken every so often for a new breath upon which to scream again. And that screaming might have been your own, but wasn't. You are paralysed, standing, staring at blank jungle through which no more than moving shadows can be seen, and yet the disembodied voices make what is happening in there all too clear. Again and again, a new voice will gasp: 'Fuck, they're your own blokes,' as the realisation dawns upon one and then another. And still the doomed man screams on and on. As you strive and fail to shut that screaming out of your brain. There is no doubt about it—you are going to have to go over there.

"Snowy? You blokes okay?"

"Yeah, we're alright. But they fuckin' ain't."

You know that. You turn back toward the company and call, louder now. "Hey, you blokes. Hold your fire," you call. "I'm coming in."

"Stay where you fuckin' are, Griffin," Bulldog Doyle booms back at you. "You and your blokes, stay away from here."

Those two voices, yours and Doyle's, so remarkably calm amid the panic that engulfs the other voices. You feel cold, shivering, covered with goose-flesh. Your entire body feels a dull ache from top to bottom. You rise and walk unsteadily, on feeble legs, across that fatal twenty-five metres. And slowly, as you advance, the scene opens up before your eyes. First the blood, splattered everywhere, and bits of other things that you will not want to investigate too closely. The men, gathered in three groups, huddling over those on the ground, and other men arrive on the scene, their faces pale with shock, while Bulldog Doyle tries to hold them back.

Your eyes are drawn first toward the screaming. The man lies on the ground, his mouth and eyes open to their extremities as that screaming went on. It is impossible to tell where his wounds might have been, such is the quantity of blood that has spilled out over those sections of his body that you can see between people's feet, and over the men bending and squatting about him, frantically striving to staunch the blood flow, to pump air through his lungs, to thump his heart back to life... Ten Days is there, up to his elbows in the redness. But the face, the face...

"For fuck's sake, shut him up," Ten Days screeches at no-one in particular. That face, that screaming face, so distorted by its efforts, and yet, for all its unrecognisability, you suddenly know that it is Mickey Wright. You turn away. It can't be true. Not poor silly Mickey left behind to point out the telephone or else he would not have been there... Close it out of your mind. Close it!

Calmly, or so it seems to you, you walk over to the next group of men, and like any ghoul at a motor accident, strain to peep over the shoulders to see what is what. The ashen face of Mumbles Dorset gazes back at you blankly, meeting your eyes and yet they look straight through you. Without changing that expression, he turns his head away. He is sitting upright, sitting on his pack as if it is a dunny seat, while men are fitting a dressing to a gaping wound in his back. He looks back then, and recognition pushes the glaze of shock from his eyes.

"You rotten bastard! You rotten bastard!" he is grunting over and over, but it is his wound he is talking about, not you. So violently does he fight his tormentors that he does not know you are there. And the final group of men, and suddenly one of them detaches himself, and strides toward you, while other men try to hold him back. Andy Kinross, with his face fixed in its most frightening sneer, bellowing at you in utter rage. "You fuckin' idiot, Yogi! I'll fuckin' kill you for this."

And you watch dumbly as he raises his SLR and points it directly at you, and you make no move to defend yourself as the weapon jerks. But nothing happens. Then you can see why, for down where the pistolgrip and trigger of the rifle should have been are only a few scraps of twisted metal and splintered wood, and even if the rifle had been workable, he still could not have used it, for he no longer has a right hand, just a stump of bloody goo that jerks convulsively as he pumps off each desperate imaginary shot. And then they had him and dragged him away.

"I'll kill you. I'll fuckin' kill you, Yogi!" he continues to roar.

Now someone bumps against you, and a hand falls roughly on your shoulder.

"Fuck you, Griffin. I told you to stay there," Bulldog Doyle roars. You turn your face toward his—to say something if you can think of something to say. And then Hatrack appears in the middle of it all and stands pointing his finger directly at you. "Get him out of here," he roars. "Get him out of here!"

Bulldog Doyle is already towing you away, his hand gripping your bicep and you are jolted into following him along. He tows you back through the jungle a little way, and again it closes around that chaotic scene and there are only the voices, all blurring in together. There is a log, or something, and Doyle sits you down upon that. You don't know how long you sit there. You remember the shape of Snowy Spargo coming at one point to stand over you, while Doyle sits alongside.

"We're all okay," Snowy murmurs, and then waits. You want to say how pleased about that you are but no words will come.

"Shock," you hear Bulldog Doyle say from a long way away. "Get something off one of the medics, will you?"

The bulk of Snowy disappears. Shock? You really don't feel that bad, not hurt or anything, not like those others guys, poor bastards, poor fuckin' Mickey...just feeling a little tired that's all. At least he's stopped screaming now, or maybe that's bad. Your head goes forward to rest upon the broad chest of Bulldog Doyle. Just for a moment, Bulldog, hope you don't mind. You can feel him put his great arm about you and there you remain until another figure, maybe Ten Days, maybe Snowy, blots out the light again. They tug at your sleeve, and you feel, vaguely, the prick of the needle going in. You stay there, your head still resting on his chest, his huge arm around you, and slowly it is all fading away. The voices further and further away, the bodies of Snowy and Doyle closing in about you and then they have closed around you completely and there is nothing at all...

13. The Last Card Game

It was the last card game, and the remnants of what was once four section of eleven platoon of Delta Company of the Pig Battalion sat around a wonky table built of dismantled packing cases in what had once been Nigel's hoochie, playing by the light of a kerosene lamp. The game, always poker, began at ten when the boozer closed and would continue through until dawn, and this time all of them had no option, no matter how drunk or tired, but to see it through to the end.

There was Snowy Spargo, retired gunner, the shearer from way out West somewhere, a simple honest hard worker but a lousy poker player because he just could not help looking pleased when he got a good hand.

"You're bluffing, Yogi."

Yogi Bear eyed him from under his ponderous brow and everything about Snowy's hand was obvious, just as everything about Snowy Spargo always was. It was Snowy who was bluffing.

"Of course I am," Griffin smiled at him cruelly.

Snowy raised the bet a couple of times but Griffin went with him without compunction. Sweat ran copiously from his brow and over his huge round shoulders, discolouring the edges of his green singlet, but the others sweated inside.

"What do I do?" Snowy asked the others.

"Give up. You can't beat him," Sniffer Gibson advised in disgust.

Snowy sighed and threw in his hand, two pairs. As a future warning, Griffin allowed them to see his full house.

"I hate you, Griffin," Snowy grumbled.

There was The Greyman, Billy Goolie, who was apparently half-white but you wouldn't have known it to look at him, and Greyman's white half cheated at poker whenever he could, but his black half would invariably look guilty and give him away.

"Three queens, I win!" he cried and his dark little hand hurled his cards into the pile before anyone could see them properly. As he tried to seize the money, Snowy slapped his wrist and then carefully extracted the cards.

"One of your Queens seems to be missing."

"Of course it fucking isn't. They're the wrong cards."

Griffin then showed his own hand—the other two Queens.

"Oh," Greyman sighed.

There were also a pair of Aces.

"Fuckin' white man's magic," Billy muttered.

There was Sniffer Gibson, the freckled lad from Tasmania whose affinity with machines was stronger than with men, and he played every hand mechanically, exactly on its merits, and always lost because no one ever won at poker that way.

"It isn't fair. I reckon if I've got the best cards, then I oughta win."

"Exactly right, Sniffer," Griffin's deep voice grumbled. "So you oughta."

"Then why don't I win when I've got a better hand than you, Yogi?"

"Ain't what you got, it's what you do with it that counts."

"Poor old Sniffer," Snowy Spargo grinned. "Been fightin' the Viet Cong for a year and still hasn't got the point."

"What's the fuckin' Viet Cong got to do with it?"

"They taught me to play poker," Griffin grinned.

"Bullshit! Charlie don't play poker."

"What he means," Snowy said patiently. "is that although our American friends have infinitely superior firepower and equipment, they are losing the war."

"Sure. No doubt about that. But what's that got to do with playing poker!"

"Just deal the fuckin' cards, Sniffer."

The fourth man was Griffin, alias Yogi the Bear, who frightened them at first the way his usually florid face was bloodless and sallow,

160

his eyes sunken hollows and his heavy forepaws shook ceaselessly as he played, and yet the great booming Bearman was still inside there somewhere, and he had become totally unbeatable at poker.

"Arr, shit, Yogi. You are the arsiest bastard I ever met."

"Not arse, Sniffer, just skill."

"Come on, Griffin," Greyman insisted. "Nobody could be this much better than everyone else at a game like poker. You are really lucky."

"If I'm so lucky, how come I got drafted?"

"I think he's got a point there," Snowy sighed.

"I've also got a king-high straight."

"Arr, shit!"

The Company had gone out on an operation that morning, but these four had been left behind. In just six weeks their time would run out and they would be returned to Australia and discharged from the army, but everyone agreed that they'd had enough, and they became permanent rear party—they didn't even really belong to a section anymore. Daytripper had been promoted to corporal and was section commander now, because he was the only experienced man left.

"Bloody Poms. Come over here and snatch all the cushy jobs," Greyman suggested.

Daytripper sighed. "And to think I might have been back home living it up in Leicester Square and missed this great career opportunity."

It became Daytripper's mob and a whole bunch of new faces filled out the numbers, for the Pig Battalion itself was not due to complete its tour for three months yet. It was as if Nigel Naughton's mob had been wiped out, but that was only on paper. The surviving members, it had been officially decided, had had enough. Snowy, Sniffer and Greyman would sit out the next three weeks like this, but Griffin would be leaving on the mail plane in the morning. It was only for him that this was the last card game.

He had returned from the hospital that morning, that ghostly quivering figure only vaguely reminiscent of his former self, and they'd kept him so drugged for all this time that he didn't really know how long it had been himself.

"I slept through the whole thing," he explained.

They knew it had been fifteen days.

He had packed and labelled his trunk and done the final paperwork at CHQ, and amongst other things, his money had been changed—that was important. In an attempt to control black market operators, the Americans issued their own currency—called scrip—for use only on its bases. Each man could carry only ten Australian dollars in or out of the country, and the US scrip had no value outside the war zone. This posed a problem for Griffin, because the money he was winning in that last card game was all US scrip and the moment he got on the plane in just a few hours, it would become worthless. Monopoly money. Each of his opponents eyed his growing pile of winnings with increasing concern.

"What are you going to do with it all?" Snowy grumbled at him.

"Take it with me," Griffin said ruthlessly.

"But it won't be worth anything," Greyman protested.

"So I'll burn it when I get home."

"Fuck you, Griffin," Sniffer lamented. "You'll send the whole base bankrupt."

"When I'm home, I won't care."

"If you get there," the others chorused.

Griffin eyed them in disgust; it was a running joke, but really they all knew that nothing could be relied upon. The mail plane could be blown out of the sky as it lifted off Nui Dat airstrip. Neither Griffin, nor any of them, could sensibly regard themselves as safe until they were actually standing on Australian soil.

The very room was pervaded by evidence of the obstacles that still lay in his path. The hourly reports from armed forces radio on Sniffer's huge transistor told them of the continuing mortar attacks on Ton Sinh Ut—Saigon International Airport—where in a matter of hours Griffin would transfer to a Qantas 707, should that still be in one piece. Ostensibly the Tet Offensive was over, but there were still pockets of resistance to be mopped up all over the country. From

162

elsewhere came reports of hundreds more NLF trapped and slaughtered. US Armed Forces Radio took you to the spot, provided only that the US forces were winning.

"There won't be any Charlies left after this," Greyman said solemnly.

"Don't bet on it," Snowy declared. "A few hundred thousand dead is a drop in the ocean to them. They breed faster than the Yanks can kill 'em."

"Do you suppose," Sniffer wondered. "if sooner or later the Yanks are gonna stop pissin' around and step on them?"

"I doubt it," Griffin said. "They just sit back inside their bases and pick them off by the hundred between their favourite TV programs. They aren't trying to win."

"Then what the fuck are we doing here?" Sniffer puzzled.

"Arse-lickin'," Snowy said emphatically. "Showin' the Yanks what good mates are, not that they give a stuff. In just one year we have cleared out Phouc Tuy Province almost entirely. Nui Dat is the only base in the whole country that they didn't attack during Tet because they didn't have enough forces left to try. And what's happening in all them other Yankee Provinces? Fuck all. They ain't tryin' to win, mate. They're just tryin' to keep the war going."

"But that's stupid!"

"Not to them," Griffin said. "Remember those terrific profits from the Arms contracts to US industry."

"Not to mention a solution to the US unemployment problem," Snowy added.

"And they get a nice handy excuse to build some enormous bases within striking distance of Russia and China."

"And then there's all that good old Yankee patriotism back home."

"This war will go on forever," Griffin said. "It might change location from time to time, but it will never end."

The Chi-Com Man lived on. When they were sure that Kinross's blokes had put an end to him, he bobbed up again a few weeks later, and continued to make his deadly nocturnal raids on a regular basis ever since. Maybe they got the wrong guy, maybe there was more than one of them, or maybe, like The Phantom, each death induced an immediate new incarnation—the ghost who walks. In their minds, all things considered, only the final possibility was likely. The Chi-Com Man, and his war, would indeed go on forever.

As would this night, and the last card game. To have all the money in the world wasn't everything, Griffin was rapidly discovering.

"Anyone got any fags?"

Sniffer offered him one.

"No, I mean a packet. I'll buy it."

"I'm running a bit short meself..."

"Ten bucks."

"Ten bucks? Jesus Christ. They way I'm losing, that ain't nothin'."

"A hundred bucks."

"You'd pay a ton for a packet of fags?"

"I can afford it. Two hundred."

"It's a deal."

Sniffer handed him a packet of Camels that were suddenly worth a dollar a puff.

"I like to get value for my money," Griffin smiled.

"How many cards do you want, you capitalist bastard."

"I'll play these."

"Arrr, shit!"

When they let him out of the hospital and he walked back into the Delta Company area—strolling with his hands in his pockets, utterly unarmed—the first person he encountered was Bulldog Doyle. The CSM sat in the Company Office with huge bandage on his hand, trying to beat himself at chess.

"Good afternoon, CSM Doyle."

"Jesus fucking Christ, Griffin. What the fuck are you doing here?"

"Nice for a bloke to feel like he belongs..."

"They said they sent you home."

"Then they know as little about where I've been as I do. What happened to your hand?"

"Got bit by a fuckin' scorpion."

"Bit of bad luck."

164

"No it wasn't. I was scratchin' me balls at the time."

Griffin laughed—it was the first time in as long as he could remember that he did that. His chest muscles seemed troubled by the unfamiliarity of it, and reduced him to a fierce coughing fit.

"You look awful, Griffin."

"I got a bit of paper here says I'm medically fit for release."

"We'll fix up your papers later," Doyle said—plainly it was all too much bother for the moment, and he waved his bandaged paw toward the four section lines. "Your blokes are over there."

"Not my blokes anymore," Griffin said, and started to walk that way. He got about three paces before Bulldog Doyle cracked.

"Griffin."

"Yeah."

"It wasn't your fault."

"Who says so, CSM?"

"I said so, in the report I had to write for Task Force."

"I appreciate the gesture, but it had to be someone's fault. Two units hit each other when they are supposed to be five hundred metres apart. Someone had to be in the wrong place."

Doyle considered his answer a long time before he made it—he was saying things that he knew he was not permitted to say. "You were in the right place. Hatrack was over-excited by the chase—you know what he was like when he was on the scent. He over-shot, that's all."

In Griffin's mind were numbers that had run through his brain a million times. "The company's bearing was 270 and I was on 274..."

But Doyle was shaking his head. "The cable changed direction—to 277 at least."

"And he didn't tell me?"

"In the heat of the moment, he didn't realise how much difference that could make. It was just an accident, Griffin."

They had an expression for it—Friendly Fire. Only the military could make so perverse a use of the word Friend. Did Mickey Wright feel better, knowing he had been killed by friends? Andy Kinross, they said, had returned to Australia where surgeons hoped to fit a hook to replace his missing hand—he didn't bother to say 'good bye' before he left. They said Mumbles Dorset lay in his hospital bed with a Browning under his pillow in case you should appear. Waiting for a friend...

"Yeah," you said. "Just an accident."

Doyle returned his attention to the chess board, and you started to walk on, but this time it was your turn to call a halt to it.

"Hey, Charlie. What was at the end of that telephone line?"

"Fuck all," Doyle said. "The little bugger cut the cord, stuck his phone under his arm, and pissed off. Couldn't have been more than two or three of them."

You breathed at the final, dismal irony of that.

"We're getting done, Charlie. These blokes are too good for us."

"Done like a dinner, Griffin. Done like the Sunday roast your old mum usta make."

"My mum," you remembered, "still does."

Four in the morning. In two hours you were going home.

"Your deal, Yogi."

Home where there was real fresh food not muck prised out of cans by cooks too drunk to tell peaches from pumpkin; home to beds with soft mattresses and clean sheets and you didn't spend the whole night sweating and listening to other men farting and pulling themselves. Home where you could take a bath, when you could go to the pub and talk to women with real breasts, not skin forced up into tight brassieres; home where the milk wasn't powdered, you craved a malted milk more than anything, and where you didn't have to carry a rifle everywhere you went.

"Hey Griffin. Deal the fuckin' cards, will ya?"

You didn't know what had happened to the AK47, your most prized possession, and hadn't troubled to ask. You didn't care. They were all here playing this last card game and no one was bothering to man the platoon picket post against enemy attack. No one cared. Everything that had been important was dissolving into inconsequence. Everything that used to matter didn't matter anymore.

You took up the cards and distributed them lethargically about the table, lit another ten dollar cigarette, and looked at your hand. Three aces. There were times when you couldn't lose, just like there were other times when you couldn't win.

"Shit, Griffin," Sniffer said. "How's your mum gonna cope when she sees the way you're always suckin' on a fag?"

"And how you're pissed out of your brain all the fuckin' time," Snowy added.

"And all yer fuckin' swearin'," Greyman put in.

It was just a tactic to try and put you off your game—although you had to admit that these thoughts had crept through your mind once or twice.

"The whole of fuckin' Moorabbin will hang its head in shame when they see what you've become," Snowy chortled on.

Griffin forced himself to grin. "I'm a war hero. They'll forgive me for everything."

Maybe not everything. There was once a simple insurance clerk from the suburbs, a good clean-living lad—didn't swear or smoke, went to church on Sundays, virginal though not for the want of trying, nice bloke. Then the army got him and turned him into an animal—hunter-killer, child-murderer, the taste of blood on his lips forever. Civilisation was bullshit—this was real. This was how those original ape-men lived, these were his most basic instincts. Kill, maim, rape, pillage. Greed and torture were the forces that drove him. Now he knew the true state of man—the most deadly predator of all, lying in ambush, waiting to slaughter the next victim. And just when he got to be good at it, they were sending him home. Try and live your nice suburban life again after this, sonny. What his nightmares saw mostly was this appalling blood-crazed primeval monster, stalking the silent leafy streets of Moorabbin.

"I have to admit it is a bit of a worry," Griffin admitted with a shiver.

"Bit of a worry, he sez," Greyman laughed. "Like the joke about the digger who arrives home first night and sits at the dinner table: Pass the fuckin' salt, he sez. Poor mum melts in shock and he realises what he's done and sez: Sorry mum, didn't mean to make a cunt of

167

meself!"

Nobody laughed, but not because it was such an old joke, but because it wasn't a joke at all.

"Alright," Griffin declared. "No more swearing. Got to practice. You each get ten bucks every time you catch me."

"Fair enough," Snowy said. "It's your deal."

"I just fuckin' dealt, you dickhead."

"Gotcha!" they shrieked and held out their hands.

"At least this way we'll have some money to get on with the game," Sniffer laughed.

It was easy to forgive them their envy. Some men had shot themselves, others prayed for wounds that would take them home, or diseases, or just for the days to pass and their time run out. To be going home was the most important thing a man could do at Nui Dat, and that was why they were sitting there with their bloodshot eyes and exhausted bodies, just trying to share a little of what you had.

What could you say to them, when you got home. How could you explain how it was? Could you really, in a pleasant suburban lounge room or the pub in Queen Street near the insurance office, tell any of them of what you did? How could you give it a context by means of which they could understand? Tell them you were a primitive predator, good only at ambushes except usually you fucked it up. Tell them about fragging and not fragging? Tell them about dead children and friendly fire? What could you say that they would understand?

Tell them a funny story maybe. About the enemy pumpkins, perhaps. Well, that one might be alright for your mum, provided you didn't explain too deeply the true purpose of an ambush. Good for a laugh. Was that all it was? The context.

No doubt you'd tell the workers in the pub about Holly's masterstroke. Early on in an operation in a very swampy region and they were losing a man a day to leeches up the prick channel, each one winched into the dust-off (really slop-off) chopper and evacuated in screaming agony, to face the even greater agony of that dreaded umbrella gadget. Too many men, but then Holly, in his naivety, came up with the solution, and ordered in on the next ration resupply, thirty gross of condoms. That would keep the little buggers out, he was sure. And so the scene of a platoon of tough combat soldiers in full fighting order, standing in a circle with their pants around their ankles, trying to fit condoms to flaccid penises, and all of them asking: "How do we get them to stay on?" and Bulldog Doyle stalking the circle roaring: "Use your imagination!"

But what of the real stories. How could you explain? They all thinking you were having a terrible time, forced to confront the horrors of war. But that wasn't the problem at all. The problem was never what they did to you, the problem was what you did to them. It wasn't the horror of war you confronted, it was yourselves.

There had been eight of you at the beginning, and now just four and only Alby Dunshea could have been attributed to the enemy. And maybe Bugsy Norris.. Certainly not Mickey Wright. And even you four no longer existed. It had been, all agreed, a hard run. Just one dead and two wounded of the original eight yet none got through to the finish. They, the survivors, fighting off the overwhelming urge to sleep a sleep that never came anyway these days, playing out this last fiasco of a card game. The survivors, or maybe they were the ones who hadn't survived.

There was a chill that told them it was first light—long familiar from their earliest army days. Just as the first light shows in the sky, the temperature drops noticeably. It was the sort of atmosphere in which the birds would have begun their morning song, had there been any of those. In their absence, Griffin detected a far off hum that was what he had been waiting for.

"Here it comes."

"What comes?"

"Can't you fuckin' hear it."

Even after the payout, it was still a few minutes before they could hear it too. The Caribou aircraft, twin-engined cargo plane, approaching Nui Dat out of the dawn. Wallaby Airlines...

"Don't crash you bastard," Griffin murmured.

169

Down on the airstrip, they heard the engines reverse as it touched down safely. All four had sat still and silent, waiting for that. Now there was time for just one more hand.

"Last chance, fellas. Do your worst."

Snowy dealt the cards and Griffin glanced at his—three kings. He pushed his entire winnings into the pot. They looked dismayed. Even after all this beating, they could still look dismayed. Griffin grinned.

"I would have done that no matter what you dealt me," he said.

"You mean we've got a chance?" Greyman asked.

"Don't be silly," he grinned.

They bought their cards with whatever they had left. Snowy laid Griffin's two face down in front of him. Griffin wondered which one was the other king—he looked at the one on the left—ten of hearts—so it had to be the one on the right. It was.

"Fuck me dead, Griffin. You are the luckiest bastard that ever lived."

"Yeah. I know."

The tent flap lifted and the feeble daylight greyed the hoochie—just enough to wither any vampires that might have been present. Bulldog Doyle stood there.

"Hullo? What's the go here?"

"G'day, Charlie. Just gettin' a few hands in before breakfast."

"You get breakfast in Vung Tau, Griffin," Doyle said. "Plane's in. Get going."

In front of Griffin was more money than he would ever again see in his life, but it was without the slightest concern that he pushed it all back into the pot.

They stared. So did Bulldog Doyle.

"I think I might just sit in for a hand or two," he said and was in the vacated chair in a stride. Griffin gathered his things while they dealt.

"Hoo Roo, boys," he called.

"See yer, Yogi," Sniffer called off-handedly.

"You won't, you know," Griffin chuckled.

"Feel free to drop in any time you're in the neighbourhood," Greyman grinned. "We're always here."

"Just make fuckin' sure you're on that plane," Snowy menaced. "We don't want to see your ugly puss around here again, got it."

"I'll take three," Bulldog Doyle said.

Griffin walked away, listening to the sounds of the last hand of the last card game, haunted by his own ghost. He walked in his new slouch hat and new starched greens and new shiny boots, carrying an overnight bag, and somehow feeling a little sad. Out over the mountains, the first rays of the rising sun showed. Down on the airstrip, men were loading the Caribou. And over to the left, a lean figure stood, familiar even if it hadn't been for the battered mug of tea in his hand. And unfamiliar too, because he had shaved off his huge moustache.

"Morning, Griffin."

"You're up early, Nigel."

"Like to get as much work done as I can before it gets too hot," said Storeman's Clerk Robert Naughton. His upper lip looked bare as the Sahara.

"Get caught in a bit of BHQ hot air," Griffin asked.

"No shortage of that, mate," he said, touching his vulnerable lip. "Against regs, you know. I heard what happened. Bastards."

"Yeah," was all Griffin said.

They stood there for a moment, two people with nothing to say to each other. This was not the Nigel you knew—not even a reasonable facsimile of him. It wasn't just the moustache, nor the BHQ clean greenness. It was as if the spark had gone, the very force that generated him, the magic that made him what he was then, but not now. Something like that. And you realised then that he probably saw you exactly the same way. Two walking dead men, standing still.

"Got a bit of news for you," he finally said.

Griffin waited on it without comment.

"They sacked Hatrack."

"They what?"

"They've kicked him upstairs to a desk job. He's already been replaced."

"Who by?"

"Donleavy. Know him."

"No."

"Worse than fuckin' Hatrack."

Griffin allowed a pause. He was going home and didn't give a stuff about Hatrack or anyone. But something worth saying finally came to mind.

"I can't understand how that man didn't get fragged."

Nigel thought about it. "He didn't because he didn't deserve it. It wasn't him we were after. It was the whole damn structure. Them politicians and arms manufacturers and fucking lying media moguls. But we couldn't get to any of them. Hatrack was as high up as we could get. That was all."

"You must have a lot of time for postmortems at BHQ."

"No matter what else happened, you used a smoke grenade, Yogi. You might have used a real one, but you didn't. Smoke grenade was right, real one was wrong. Simple as that."

"Just a fuckin' game, isn't it."

"You better watch your language when you get home, Private Griffin."

The plane was loaded. It was time to go. But you didn't. There was one more thing to be said, and at last you knew what it was.

"How was it, Nigel, that after all that trying, we got that ambush right just once, and then buggered it up every time after that."

"Yeah, thought about that too. I guess maybe that after we got it right once, we never wanted to get it right again."

"That's pretty deep, Nigel."

"Get outa here, Yogi."

"Still, we did alright for a bit there."

"You sure?"

"No. You're right. It was a fuckin' fiasco, wasn't it."

"The whole bloody thing's a fuckin' fiasco, Yogi."

The pilot was calling, and a helmeted crewman running over to direct Griffin onto the plane. He turned and jogged through the dust blasted up by the engines. The crewman found him a seat on a box and he could look out a porthole and see Nigel standing there, still clutching his mug, and then he raised it to Griffin and Griffin waved back. The engines roared louder and the plane swung around and he watched the rows of rubber trees go by until they blurred and then began to fall away below. He might have felt a little sad, but he felt bloody good as well. At least no one would call him Bear names anymore.

Black Pepper TITLES

Black Pepper titles are available from good bookstores or may be ordered directly from the publisher: 403 St Georges Road, North Fitzroy, 3068. tel 9489 1716 Fax 9489 5318.
Catalogues are available on request.

SPECIAL EDITIONS

In 1999, in recognition of the quality of its titles *Black Pepper* launched the Special Editions range of poetry and fiction. These titles are unique in that each book of the first edition is individually signed and numbered by the author.

THE *Black Pepper* CLUB

Set up in the year 2000, The Black Pepper Club offers members advance notification of all new Black Pepper titles, giving them first option to purchase the limited signed and numbered first editions.

Other benefits are pre-publication discounts, invitations to Black Pepper book launches and the Black Pepper Christmas Party, and discounts on backlist titles. (All Black Pepper mail order prices include postage within Australia.)

Membership is free: to join write, fax, or phone Black Pepper at the address above.

FICTION

BY WAY OF WATER Phil Leask

A PICTURE OUT OF FRAME Mammad Aidani

KICKING IN DANGER Alan Wearne

LETTERS FROM BYRON Jim Williams

AND THE WINNER IS... Jon Weaving

THE SET UP John Vasilakakos

NAVIGATIO Alison Croggon

GIFTS & SORROWS Raphaelle Pomian

MEDITATIONS OF A FLAWED GROOM Vivian Hopkirk

DIARY OF A DWARF Graham Henderson

SAILING THROUGH THE AMBER Susan Hancock

THE PRISONER GAINS A BLURRED SKIN Nicholas Playford

POETRY

CORK & OTHER POEMS Louis de Paor

DEAR B Jennifer Harrison

MELBOURNE ELEGIES K. F. Pearson

THE GENIUS OF HUMAN IMPERFECTION Jack Hibberd

THE HANGING OF JEAN LEE Jordie Albiston

ALBUM OF DOMESTIC EXILES Andrew Sant

THE SHADOW'S KEEP John Anderson

FILTH AND OTHER POEMS Hugh Tolhurst

THE BLUE GATE Alison Croggon

THE WILD REPLY Emma Lew

BOTANY BAY DOCUMENT Jordie Albiston

CABRAMATTA/CUDMIRRAH Jennifer Harrison

THE APPARITION'S DAYBOOK K. F. Pearson

SENTENCES OF EARTH AND STONE Louis De Paor

THE FOREST SET OUT LIKE THE NIGHT John Anderson

MOSAICS & MIRRORS Jennifer Harrison, Graham Henderson and K. F. Pearson

AN AUSTRALIAN CONFERENCE OF THE BIRDS Anne Fairbairn

PASSION & WAR K. F. Pearson

MICHELANGELO'S PRISONERS Jennifer Harrison